Roads to New Delhi

Ruskin Bond has been writing for over sixty years, and now has over 120 titles in print—novels, collections of short stories, poetry, essays, anthologies and books for children. His first novel, *The Room on the Roof*, received the prestigious John Llewellyn Rhys Prize in 1957. He has also received the Padma Shri (1999), the Padma Bhushan (2014) and two awards from Sahitya Akademi—one for his short stories and another for his writings for children. In 2012, the Delhi government gave him its Lifetime Achievement Award.

Born in 1934, Ruskin Bond grew up in Jamnagar, Shimla, New Delhi and Dehradun. Apart from three years in the UK, he has spent all his life in India, and now lives in Mussoorie with his adopted family.

RUSKIN BOND
Roads to New Delhi

RUPA

Published by
Rupa Publications India Pvt. Ltd 2021
161-B/4, Gulmohar House,
Yusuf Sarai Community Centre,
New Delhi 110049

Sales centres:
Bengaluru Chennai
Hyderabad Kolkata Mumbai

Copyright © Ruskin Bond, 2021

This is a work of fiction. Names, characters, places and incidents are either the product of the author's imagination or are used fictitiously and any resemblance to any actual person, living or dead, events or locales is entirely coincidental.

All rights reserved.
No part of this publication may be reproduced, transmitted, or stored in a retrieval system, in any form or by any means, electronic, mechanical, photocopying, recording or otherwise, without the prior permission of the publisher.

P-ISBN: 978-93-90918-09-6
E-ISBN: 978-93-90918-17-1

Eighth impression 2026

10 9 8

The moral right of the author has been asserted.

Printed in India

This book is sold subject to the condition that it shall not, by way of trade or otherwise, be lent, resold, hired out, or otherwise circulated, without the publisher's prior consent, in any form of binding or cover other than that in which it is published.

CONTENTS

Introduction   *vii*

1. Walking the Streets of Delhi   1
2. Bhabiji's House   11
3. Chachi's Funeral   25
4. The Last Time I Saw Delhi   29
5. Untouchable   35
6. The Flute Player   41
7. Hanging at the Mango Tope   51
8. A Man Called Brain   57
9. Susanna's Seven Husbands   66
10. Street of the Red Well   73
11. Footloose in Agra   77
12. The Daryaganj Strangler   87
13. Reunion at the Regal   100

INTRODUCTION

I first saw New Delhi in 1942, five years before Independence, and last saw it in March of 2020, just before the Covid-19 epidemic spread throughout the world. And so, as you can imagine, I have seen our capital grow and change considerably over the years.

The historians can tell you about the seven cities of Delhi that existed before New Delhi came into being; the ruins of past empires are still scattered about the city. When, at the age of eight, I came to live with my father in an R.A.F. hutment on Humayun Road. World War II was in progress and so was the Quit India movement.

As a child I was not greatly impacted by these events, and I have fond memories of all that Connaught Place could offer by way of cinemas, milk bars, pastry shops and bookshops, for I had an indulgent and loving father who did his best to make me happy.

My father died before the war was over, and many years were to pass before I lived in New Delhi again. It wasn't until 1958 that I found myself a Delhi resident once more, but now living on the outskirts, in one of those far-flung refugee colonies that are now an integral part of the city. I was a Delhi-ite for five years before I made my great escape to the hills and a life of full-time writing.

As the reader knows, most of my stories have been set in hill stations or verdant valleys, but occasionally I have reminisced about my time in New (and old) Delhi, and I have put together this selection of stories and essays to give the reader some idea of what life was like in the capital some 60 years ago!

In recent years I have often visited New Delhi, because that is where book publishers abound. At one time, they were all concentrated in Daryaganj, but now you will find them scattered in Noida, Gurgaon, and once romantic spots such as Yusuf Sarai. I enjoy my trips to Delhi, especially the six-hour road journey from Dehradun, and I hope it won't be long before I'm crossing the sluggish but familiar Yamuna, and catching sight of a constantly changing city.

Ruskin Bond

WALKING THE STREETS OF DELHI

I made my home in Mussoorie in 1963, but of course I was to revisit Delhi many times, even spending a couple of winters there.

On one of these visits, in 1971, I reached my friend Kamal's house in Rajouri Garden, and mentioned that I had walked from Connaught Place, a distance of some eight miles. His family greeted me with a pained and bewildered silence.

Finally my friend's mother, a practical Punjabi lady, asked: 'How did you lose your money?' She kept hers knotted in the end of her sari, and firmly believed that people who kept their money in easily snatched handbags and wallets were asking for trouble.

'I haven't lost anything,' I said.

'Aren't the buses running?'

'Oh, the buses are running. One nearly ran over me.'

'Then why did you walk?'

'I thought I'd see more that way.'

The rest of the story is told in my journal.

The consensus of opinion in my friend's house is that I am a little mad. They have never heard of anyone in Delhi walking from choice. They prefer to wait long periods for overcrowded buses and hang on by their eyebrows, even if the distance to be covered is only a furlong. As in big cities the world over, the people of Delhi are rapidly losing the use of their legs.

I suppose Delhi is one of the least attractive cities in which to walk about. Crossing roads can be hazardous. Single and double-decker buses (many emitting smokescreens of diesel fumes), wildly driven taxis, unpredictable scooter-rickshaws, slow-moving cars and tongas, and thousands of wavering, wayward cyclists, make for chaos on the streets. On the main roads the traffic is fast and furious, and cyclists are frequently knocked over and killed. But Delhi has an acute transport problem, and the cycle is the poor man's only guarantee of getting to work in time. He cannot afford a scooter, and he cannot wait for a bus. And yet, in this city bursting with the Punjabi nouveau riche there are thousands who do have their own scooters and cars, and the number and variety of vehicles on the road increase at an alarming rate.

Setting out on another long walk, I realized that the pavement is meant for almost every purpose except walking. I am on the Najafgarh Road, heading in the general direction of central Delhi. It is a straight road, but this is no straight walk. To find a thirty-yard stretch of unoccupied pavement is most unlikely. In a territory where every square foot of land has a high price, why should so much good pavement go to waste?

The first two wayside stalls belong to sellers of lottery tickets. Theirs is a thriving business. All over Delhi, at almost every street corner, there is someone selling lottery tickets. The prizes are attractive enough. The owner of the winning ticket collects ₹250,000—sometimes more—and there are a number of other prizes. And the income accruing to the state is also tremendous—so much so that almost every state in the country, including Delhi, has climbed on the lottery bandwagon. After all, it is easier than collecting taxes. No one, not even the street sweeper, grudges giving a rupee to the government if there is a chance in a million of his winning a fortune.

While the poor man is quite willing to part with his rupee, it is the rich man, the thriving businessman, who often goes in for lottery tickets in a big way, sometimes buying up forty or fifty tickets at a time. He believes that while it is great to be rich, there is nothing like getting richer.

How times have changed. Ten years ago, if I asked a Sikh boy what he would like to be on growing up, he would unhesitatingly have said, 'I'll join the Army'—or the Navy, or the Air Force. He was proud of his martial traditions. Yesterday, while talking to an intelligent twelve-year-old Sikh, I asked the same question and received this reply: 'I'll open a cinema or deal in spare parts.'

No spirit of adventure, no vision of faraway places—unless it be of a cloth shop in Bangkok! The boy confessed that what he really wanted in life was a television set bigger and better than his neighbour's.

But Delhi is not entirely Punjabi. Here, on the Najafgarh Road I find a community of Lohiawalas, a gypsy tribe of blacksmiths who have wandered into Delhi, camped on the pavement, and gone about their ancient and traditional way of living, supremely indifferent to the fast pace, the noise of traffic, the neon signs and Western clothes that surround them on all sides. Their bullock-carts (in which they travel and sleep and live and die and have their babies) stand just off the pavement; these are lined with old iron, stamped with decorative patterns and studded with coloured stones.

A charcoal fire has been made in a hole in the ground, and this is kept alive by a bellows worked by a wheel turned by an attractive woman wearing a black blouse and black skirt. This sombre attire is set off by heavy silver anklets and a pair of very lively eyes. Another pair of bellows has been fashioned out of goat's skin. A man is beating out a strip of red-hot tin on his anvil. A boy is filling a bent bicycle-pump with sand (to keep it firm) before straightening it out with his hammer. The entire family, including bearded old men, wizened old women ready to take off on broomsticks, and naked grandchildren, is at work. Handsome people these; and although they live in dirt and squalor, they seem quiet and dignified.

A little farther along the road are some people making what appear to be straw mats. These turn out to be roofs for the small shacks belonging to the Rajasthani labourers who live on the other side of an open drain. The walls of these shacks are about four feet high, the rooms about six feet square. There is no sanitation. People use the drain. They bathe at a public tap. During the rains, water moves sluggishly along this drain, but now it is dry except for pools of stagnant, slimy water, a grey liquid tinged with green. It must hold treasures for anyone searching for biological specimens. (And indeed, the enterprising Delhiwala has not ignored this possibility, for farther along, on Link Road, frogs are on sale to biology students.)

At this side of the road lies a dead pony, knocked down at night by a speeding truck. A portion has been eaten away by dogs and jackals. It is now being pecked at by crows; when these birds tire of the stinking carcass they move on to a nearby fruit stall. No one seems to notice this, least of all the fruit vendors. Well-dressed people pass by without a glance at the dead horse or the open drain. Is it apathy, or is it that Delhi people—city people—are unobservant by nature? Does city life dull the perceptions? Are the giant cinema hoardings so overpowering, so dazzling, that everything else pales into insignificance beside them?

Some of the shack-dwellers have tried to make their homes attractive. They have whitewashed their walls, adorned them with crude but colourful drawings of birds and animals. But what a contrast there is between these humble homes and the elegant villas and bungalows of Kirti Nagar, Patel Nagar and Pusa Road, three prosperous areas of Delhi which lie on my route. A tenant has to pay anything from three to five hundred rupees a month for a small flat in one of these fine houses.

I went flat-hunting once, but I was turned away by the house-owners—not because of race, colour or religion, but because I was a bachelor. In India, staying single is something of a crime against society. Bachelors have a rough time;

they seldom get invited into homes where there are girls of marriageable age.

'Are Delhi bachelors such monsters?' I asked a house agent in Rajinder Nagar.

'Most of them are very well-behaved,' he said. 'But you see, parents no longer have much confidence in their daughters. A girl sees too many films, and then she wants to have a tragic affair with the first good-looking male who comes along.'

It has taken me two hours of foot-slogging to reach Connaught Place, which is still the premier shopping centre of New Delhi, I remember it well from my childhood, in the war years, when my father was stationed at Air Headquarters in New Delhi. The capital was a small, sparsely populated town in those days. We lived in temporary RAF hutments on Wellesley Road. A multi-storeyed hotel now occupies the site. The jungle where I hunted rabbits has long since been cleared to make way for the expensive residential area of Sunder Nagar. But the central vista, leading from India Gate up to Lutyens's complex of Parliament House and the President's Estate, is still a lovely stretch of green grass, still water and shady jamun trees.

Connaught Place has not changed much. The milk bar I frequented as a boy is still there, although they do not sell milk any more; now it is espresso coffee and hamburgers. The Regal cinema has switched over to Hindi films. In its cellar is a discotheque. Shopfronts are more flashy, but service-lanes have not altered. And of course the faces and clothes are different. The British uniforms of the war years have given way to the uniforms of the hippies, who slouch about in beads and togas, unaccepted and even scorned by the local citizens. Indians are not impressed by people who do not dress well. Their concept of the true Englishman is of the sahib who dresses for dinner even when there is no dinner; they *like* that kind of Englishman. No one is as clothes-conscious as a Punjabi. He likes his shoes polished, his shirt pressed, his suit spotless—a difficult business in Delhi, where the dust, even in winter, is as thick as in the time of Emperor Shah Jahan who, proud of his new capital, asked the Persian Ambassador how it compared with his Isphahan, and received the double-edged reply: 'By God! Isphahan cannot be compared with the dust of your Delhi!'

But Shah Jahan's Delhi, the old walled city near the Yamuna, is not on my route today. I am tired and hungry, and I lunch at a dhaba, a cheap eating-house, one of many lining the outer pavements round Connaught Place. If one does not mind the filthy surroundings, there is good meat to be had in these little restaurants, most of them run by Punjabis who learned their cooking in Lahore. Certainly the food here is better and cheaper than the watered-down dishes served in some of the smart restaurants in the inner circle. The dish-washers and servers are barefooted hill boys, working in the city because their small fields in the hills do not provide a sufficient living for their families. They work quite cheerfully (for they are cheerful by nature), in spite of hard words, cuffs and meagre wages.

Outside, on the road, a small crowd has gathered round a turbaned Pathan. For a moment I fear violence for this exotic stranger; then I realize that the crowd is merely curious, even in good humour. The Pathan is extolling the virtues of an aphrodisiac mixture which he is trying to sell. 'Be happy!' he cries. 'And make your bulbul happy!'

In spite of the family planning hoarding directly behind him, he appears to be doing good business. It is, after all, the wedding season.

I am forcibly reminded of this on my way home in the evening. The roads in and out of every residential area are blocked by shamianas put up for wedding receptions. This is illegal, but the fine is a small one, and when a father is spending thousands on his daughter's wedding, he dosen't mind paying a fine of forty rupees. He accepts the summons with good humour, and carries on with the reception. This is the month most propitious for marriages. After 15 January, four months must pass before a Hindu will marry off his daughter. Astrology plays as great a part in the lives of the people here today as it did three hundred years ago when the traveller Francois Bernier observed that no one in Delhi, Hindu or Muslim, undertook any project without first consulting his astrologer. Today, matchmakers must still study the stars in their courses before pairing a boy with a girl.

Most fathers love to give their daughters a good send-off, and Delhi marriages are splendid, glittering affairs. The bridegroom traditionally arrives on a white horse, but Delhiwalas, who like being up-to-date, often use cars, jeeps or even tractors (because of the high perch they provide).

I find myself involved in a procession on Pusa Road. It is impossible to get past the throng of people, so I must remain with them for some distance. If I choose to attend the reception, no one will turn me away. The bride's people will be under the impression that I am one of the bridegroom's guests, and the bridegroom's group will feel sure that I belong to the bride's party. As most of the guests are seeing each other for the first time, it is possible for any well-dressed person to join the festivities. This frequently happens.

There has, of course, to be a band, and bands are chosen mainly on the strength of the volume of noise they are able to produce and sustain. A trumpet, sounding a foot away from my ear, sends me reeling to the rear of the procession. Drums, bugles, clarinets and saxophones burst into a great profanity of sound. It is not Indian music they play, but a combination of military marches and popular Hindi film tunes. There is nothing like it anywhere else on earth.

The bandsmen wear red coats and white spats, but shoes are optional. On their heads they wear what appear to be Salvation Army caps. They will play on their instruments (often independently of each other) for as long as they are paid to play, and must deliver a final burst at daybreak when the bride leaves her father's house.

It is a colourful procession, headed by small urchin boys carrying gas lamps. After them comes the band; then the bridegroom's beautifully clothed friends and relatives; and finally the bridegroom, enthroned on top of a gaily caparisoned jeep.

I take a side road and leave the procession, but find my way blocked by another marriage party. This time a heavily-built Sikh, slightly tipsy, embraces me as a long-lost brother.

He seems to know me. Quite possibly I knew him when he was a smooth-cheeked lad of fifteen; but now, disguised by a magnificent beard, he reminds me of no one I have ever known. But he wants me to join his party, and so, to humour him, I accompany him for about a hundred yards, when he suddenly forgets me and rushes off to some other old acquaintance.

I have to reconnoitre another three processions, and four more shamianas, before I reach Rajouri Garden. I keep going by eating boiled eggs. These are sold on the roadside, and the egg-seller will even peel the egg for you, and serve it sliced, with pepper and salt, on a piece of newspaper. Unfortunately all the egg-sellers disappear when summer comes, because people believe that eggs are 'heating' and should only be eaten during the winter months. I suppose the same reasoning applies to the Pathan's tonic mixture. I am almost home. It does not look as though anyone in Delhi sleeps at night, but I am ready for bed, and all the brass bands in the city (and there must be over a hundred of them) will not keep me from sleeping.

But there is something I must do first.

The seller of lottery tickets has been staring hopefully at me, and I hate to disappoint him last thing at night. So I produce a rupee and buy a ticket; and, in doing so, I feel that I have finally identified myself with the good people of Delhi.

BHABIJI'S HOUSE

My neighbours in Rajouri Garden back in the 1960s were the Kamal family. This entry from my journal, which I wrote on one of my later visits, describes a typical day in that household.

At first light there is a tremendous burst of birdsong from the guava tree in the little garden. Over a hundred sparrows wake up all at once and give tongue to whatever it is that sparrows have to say to each other at five o'clock on a foggy winter's morning in Delhi.

In the small house, people sleep on; that is, everyone except 'Bhabiji'—Granny—the head of the lively Punjabi middle-class family with whom I nearly always stay when I am in Delhi.

She coughs, stirs, groans, grumbles and gets out of bed. The fire has to be lit, and food prepared for two of her sons to take to work. There is her daughter-in-law, Shobha, to help her; but the girl is not very bright at getting up in the morning. Actually, it is this way: Bhabiji wants to show up her daughter-in-law; so, no matter how hard Shobha tries to be up first, Bhabiji forestalls her. The old lady does not sleep well, anyway; her eyes are open long before the first sparrow chirps, and as soon as she sees her daughter-in-law stirring, she scrambles out of bed and hurries to the kitchen. This gives her the opportunity to say: 'What good is a daughter-in-law when I have to get up to prepare her husband's food?'

The truth is that Bhabiji does not like anyone else preparing her sons' food. She looks no older than when I first saw her ten years ago. She still has complete control over a large family and, with tremendous confidence and enthusiasm, presides over the lives of three sons, a daughter, two daughters-in-law and fourteen grandchildren. This is a joint family (there are not many left in a big city like Delhi), in which the sons and their families all live together as one unit under their mother's benevolent (and sometimes slightly malevolent) autocracy. Even when her husband was alive, Bhabiji dominated the household.

The eldest son, Shiv, has a separate kitchen, but his wife and children participate in all the family celebrations and quarrels. It is a small miracle how everyone (including myself when I visit) manages to fit into the house; and a stranger might be forgiven for wondering where everyone sleeps, for no beds are visible during the day. That is because the beds—light wooden frames with rough string across—are brought in only at night, and are taken out first thing in the morning and kept in the garden shed.

As Bhabiji lights the kitchen fire, the household begins to stir, and Shobha joins her mother-in-law in the kitchen. As a guest I am privileged and may get up last. But my bed soon becomes an island battered by waves of scurrying, shouting children, eager to bathe, dress, eat and find their school books. Before I can get up, someone brings me a tumbler of hot sweet tea. It is a brass tumbler and burns my fingers; I have yet to learn how to hold one properly. Punjabis like their tea with lots of milk and sugar—so much so that I often wonder why they bother to add any tea.

Ten years ago, 'bed tea' was unheard of in Bhabiji's house. Then, the first time I came to stay, Kamal, the youngest son, told Bhabiji: 'My friend is Angrez. He must have tea in bed.' He forgot to mention that I usually took my morning cup at seven; they gave it to me at five. I gulped it down and went to sleep again. Then, slowly, others in the household began indulging in morning cups of tea. Now everyone, including the older children, has 'bed tea'. They bless my English forebears for instituting the custom; I bless the Punjabis for perpetuating it.

Breakfast is by rota, in the kitchen. It is a tiny room and accommodates only four adults at a time. The children have eaten first; but the smallest children, Shobha's toddlers, keep coming in and climbing over us. Says Bhabiji of the youngest and most mischievous: 'He lives only because God keeps a special eye on him.'

Kamal, his elder brother Arun and I sit cross-legged and barefooted on the floor while Bhabiji serves us hot parathas stuffed with potatoes and onions, along with omelettes, an excellent dish. Arun then goes to work on his scooter, while Kamal catches a bus for the city, where he attends an art college. After they have gone, Bhabiji and Shobha have their breakfast.

By nine o'clock everyone who is still in the house is busy doing something. Shobha is washing clothes. Bhabiji has settled down on a cot with a huge pile of spinach, which she methodically cleans and chops up. Madhu, her fourteen-year-old granddaughter, who attends school only in the afternoons, is washing down the sitting room floor. Madhu's mother is a teacher in a primary school in Delhi, and earns a pittance of Rs 150 a month. Her husband went to England ten years ago, and never returned; he does not send any money home.

Madhu is made attractive by the gravity of her countenance. She is always thoughtful, reflective; seldom speaks, smiles rarely (but looks very pretty when she does). I wonder what she thinks about as she scrubs floors, prepares meals with Bhabiji, washes dishes and even finds a few hard-pressed moments for her schoolwork. She is the Cinderella of the house. Not that she has to put up with anything like a cruel stepmother. Madhu is Bhabiji's favourite. She has made herself so useful that she is above all reproach. Apart from that, there is a certain measure of aloofness about her—she does not get involved in domestic squabbles—and this is foreign to a household in which everyone has something to say for himself or herself. Her two young brothers are constantly being reprimanded; but no one says anything to Madhu. Only yesterday morning, when clothes were being washed and Madhu was scrubbing the floor, the following dialogue took place.

Madhu's mother (picking up a school book left in the courtyard): 'Where's that boy Popat? See how careless he is with his books! Popat! He's run off. Just wait till he gets back. I'll give him a good beating.'

Vinod's mother: 'It's not Popat's book. It's Vinod's. Where's Vinod?'

Vinod (grumpily): 'It's Madhu's book.'

Silence for a minute or two. Madhu continues scrubbing the floor; she does not bother to look up. Vinod picks up the book and takes it indoors. The women return to their chores.

Manju, daughter of Shiv and sister of Vinod, is averse to housework and, as a result, is always being scolded—by her parents, grandmother, uncles and aunts.

Now, she is engaged in the unwelcomed chore of sweeping the front yard. She does this with a sulky look, ignoring my cheerful remarks. I have been sitting under the guava tree, but Manju soon sweeps me away from this spot. She creates a drifting cloud of dust, and seems satisfied only when the dust settles on the clothes that have just been hung up to dry. Manju is a sensuous creature and like most sensuous people, is lazy by nature. She does not like sweeping because the boy next door can see her at it, and she wants to appear before him in a more glamorous light. Her first action every morning is to turn to the cinema advertisements in the newspaper. Bombay's movie moguls cater for girls like Manju who long to be tragic heroines. Life is so very dull for middle-class teenagers in Delhi that it is only natural that they should lean so heavily on escapist entertainment. Every residential area has a cinema. But there is not a single bookshop in this particular suburb, although it has a population of over twenty thousand literate people. Few children read books; but they are adept at swotting up examination 'guides'; and students of, say, Hardy or Dickens read the guides and not the novels.

Bhabiji is now grinding onions and chillies in a mortar. Her eyes are watering but she is in a good mood. Shobha sits quietly in the kitchen. A little while ago she was complaining to me of a backache. I am the only one who lends a sympathetic ear to complaints of aches and pains. But since last night, my sympathies have been under severe strain. When I got into bed at about ten o'clock, I found the sheets wet. Apparently Shobha had put her baby to sleep in my bed during the afternoon.

While the housework is still in progress, cousin Kishore arrives. He is an itinerant musician who makes a living by arranging performances at weddings. He visits Bhabiji's house frequently and at odd hours, often a little tipsy, always brimming over with goodwill and grandiose plans for the future. It was once his ambition to be a film producer, and some years back he lost a lot of Bhabiji's money in producing a film that was never completed. He still talks of finishing it.

'Brother,' he says, taking me into his confidence for the hundredth time, 'do you know anyone who has a movie camera?'

'No,' I say, knowing only too well how these admissions can lead me into a morass of complicated manoeuvres. But Kishore is not easily put off, especially when he has been fortified with country liquor.

'But you *knew* someone with a movie camera?' he asks.

'That was long ago.'

'How long ago?' (I have got him going now.)

'About five years back.'

'Only five years? Find him, find him!'

'It's no use. He doesn't have the movie camera any more. He sold it.'

'Sold it!' Kishore looks at me as though I have done him an injury. 'But why didn't you buy it? All we need is a movie camera, and our fortune is made. I will produce the film, I will direct it, I will write the music. Two in one, Charlie Chaplin and Raj Kapoor. Why didn't you buy the camera?'

'Because I didn't have the money.'

'But we could have borrowed the money.'

'If you are in a position to borrow money, you can go out and buy another movie camera.'

'We could have borrowed the camera. Do you know anyone else who has one?'

'Not a soul.' I am firm this time; I will not be led into another maze.

'Very sad, very sad,' mutters Kishore. And with a dejected, hangdog expression designed to make me feel that I am responsible for all his failures, he moves off.

Bhabiji had expressed some annoyance at his arrival, but he softens her up by leaving behind an invitation to a wedding party this evening. No one in the house knows the bride's or bridegroom's family, but that does not matter; knowing one of the musicians is just as good. Almost everyone will go.

While Bhabiji, Shobha and Madhu are preparing lunch, Bhabiji engages in one of her favourite subjects of conversation, Kamal's marriage, which she hopes she will be able to arrange in the near future. She freely acknowledges that she made grave blunders in selecting wives for her other sons—this is meant to be heard by Shobha—and promises not to repeat her mistakes. According to Bhabiji, Kamal's bride should be both educated and domesticated; and of course she must be fair.

'What if he likes a dark girl?' I ask teasingly.

Bhabiji looks horrified. 'He cannot marry a dark girl,' she declares.

'But dark girls are beautiful,' I tell her.

'Impossible!'

'Do you want him to marry a European girl?'

'No foreigners! I know them, they'll take my son away. He shall have a good Punjabi girl, with a complexion the colour of wheat.'

Noon. The shadows shift and cross the road. I sit beneath the guava tree and watch the women at work. They will not let me do anything, but they like talking to me and they love to hear my broken Punjabi. Sparrows flit about at their feet, snapping up the grain that runs away from their busy fingers. A crow looks speculatively at the empty kitchen, sidles towards the open door; but Bhabiji has only to glance up and the experienced crow flies away. He knows he will not be able to make off with anything from this house.

One by one the children come home, demanding food. Now it is Madhu's turn to go to school. Her younger brother Popat, an intelligent but undersized boy of thirteen, appears in the doorway and asks for lunch.

'Be off!' says Bhabiji. 'It isn't ready yet.'

Actually the food is ready and only the chapatis remain to be made. Shobha will attend to them. Bhabiji lies down on her cot in the sun, complaining of a pain in her back and ringing noises in her ears.

'I'll press your back,' says Popat. He has been out of Bhabiji's favour lately, and is looking for an opportunity to be rehabilitated.

Barefooted, he stands on Bhabiji's back and treads her weary flesh and bones with a gentle walking-in-one-spot movement. Bhabiji grunts with relief. Every day she has new pains in new places. Her age, and the daily business of feeding the family and running everyone's affairs, are beginning to tell on her. But she would sooner die than give up her position of dominance in the house. Her working sons still hand over their pay to her, and she dispenses the money as she sees fit.

The pummelling she gets from Popat puts her in a better mood, and she holds forth on another favourite subject, the respective merits of various dowries. Shiv's wife (according to Bhabiji) brought nothing with her but a string cot; Kishore's wife brought only a sharp and clever tongue; Shobha brought a wonderful steel cupboard, fully expecting that it would do all the housework for her.

This last observation upsets Shobha, and a little later I find her under the guava tree, weeping profusely. I give her the comforting words she obviously expects; but it is her husband Arun who will have to bear the brunt of her outraged feelings when he comes home this evening. He is rather nervous of his wife. Last night he wanted to eat out, at a restaurant, but did not want to be accused of wasting money; so he stuffed fifteen rupees into my pocket and asked me to invite both him and Shobha to dinner, which I did.

We had a good dinner. Such unexpected hospitality on my part has further improved my standing with Shobha. Now, in spite of other chores, she sees that I get cups of tea and coffee at odd hours of the day.

Bhabiji knows Arun is soft with his wife, and taunts him about it. She was saying this morning that whenever there is any work to be done Shobha retires to bed with a headache (partly true). She says even Manju does more housework (not true). Bhabiji has certain talents as an actress, and does a good take-off of Shobha sulking and grumbling at having too much to do.

While Bhabiji talks, Popat sneaks off and goes for a ride on the bicycle. It is a very old bicycle and is constantly undergoing repairs. 'The soul has gone out of it,' says Vinod philosophically and makes his way on to the roof, where he keeps a store of pornographic literature. Up there, he cannot be seen and cannot be remembered, and so avoids being sent out on errands.

One of the boys is bathing at the handpump. Manju, who should have gone to school with Madhu, is stretched out on a cot, complaining of fever. But she will be up in time to attend the wedding party…

Towards evening, as the birds return to roost in the guava tree, their chatter is challenged by the tumult of people in the house getting ready for the wedding party.

Manju presses her tight pyjamas but neglects to darn them. She wears a loose-fitting, diaphanous shirt. She keeps flitting in and out of the front room so that I can admire the way she glitters. Shobha has used too much powder and lipstick in an effort to look like the femme fatale which she indubitably is not. Shiv's more conservative wife floats around in loose, old-fashioned pyjamas. Bhabiji is sober and austere in a white sari. Madhu looks neat. The men wear their suits.

Popat is holding up a mirror for his Uncle Kishore, who is combing his long hair. (Kishore kept his hair long, like a court musician at the time of Akbar, before the hippies had been heard of.) He is nodding benevolently, having fortified himself from a bottle labelled 'Som Ras' ('Nectar of the Gods'), obtained cheaply from an illicit still.

Kishore: 'Don't shake the mirror, boy!'

Popat: 'Uncle, it's your head that's shaking.'

Shobha is happy. She loves going out, especially to weddings, and she always takes her two small boys with her, although they invariably spoil the carpets.

Only Kamal, Popat and I remain behind. I have had more than my share of wedding parties.

The house is strangely quiet. It does not seem so small now, with only three people left in it. The kitchen has been locked (Bhabiji will not leave it open while Popat is still in the house), so we visit the dhaba, the wayside restaurant near the main road, and this time I pay the bill with my own money. We have kababs and chicken curry.

Yesterday, Kamal and I took our lunch on the grass of the Buddha Jayanti Gardens (Buddha's Birthday Gardens). There was no college for Kamal, as the majority of Delhi's students had hijacked a number of corporation buses and headed for the Pakistan High Commission, with every intention of levelling it to the ground if possible, as a protest against the hijacking of an Indian plane from Srinagar to Lahore. The students were met by the Delhi police in full strength, and a pitched battle took place, in which stones from the students and tear gas shells from the police were the favoured missiles. There were two shells fired every minute, according to a newspaper report. And this went on all day. A number of students and policemen were injured, but by some miracle no one was killed. The police held their ground, and the Pakistan High Commission remained inviolate. But the Australian High Commission, situated to the rear of the student brigade, received most of the tear gas shells, and had to close down for the day.

Kamal and I attended the siege for about an hour, before retiring to the Gardens with our ham sandwiches. A couple of friendly squirrels came up to investigate and were soon taking bread from our hands. We could hear the chanting of the students in the distance. I lay back on the grass and opened my copy of *Barchester Towers*. Whenever life in Delhi, or in Bhabiji's house (or anywhere, for that matter), becomes too tumultuous, I turn to Trollope. Nothing could be further removed from the turmoil of our times than an English cathedral town in the nineteenth century. But I think Jane Austen would have appreciated life in Bhabiji's house.

By ten o'clock, everyone is back from the wedding. (They had gone for the feast, and not for the ceremonies, which continue into the early hours of the morning.) Shobha is full of praise for the bridegroom's good looks and fair complexion. She describes him as being 'gora-chitta'—very white! She does not have a high opinion of the bride.

Shiv, in a happy and reflective mood, extols the qualities of his own wife, referring to her as the Barrel. He tells us how, shortly after their marriage, she had threatened to throw a brick at the next-door girl. This little incident remains fresh in Shiv's mind, after eighteen years of marriage.

He says: 'When the neighbours came and complained, I told them, "It is quite possible that my wife will throw a brick at your daughter. She is in the habit of throwing bricks." The neighbours held their peace.'

I think Shiv is rather proud of his wife's militancy when it comes to taking on neighbours; recently she vanquished the woman next door (a formidable Sikh lady) after a verbal battle that lasted three hours. But in arguments or quarrels with Bhabiji, Shiv's wife always loses, because Shiv takes his mother's side. Arun, on the other hand, is afraid of both wife and mother, and simply makes himself scarce when a quarrel develops. Or he tells his mother she is right, and then, to placate Shobha, takes her to the pictures.

Kishore turns up just as everyone is about to go to bed. Bhabiji is annoyed at first, because he has been drinking too much; but when he produces a bunch of cinema tickets, she is mollified and asks him to stay the night. Not even Bhabiji likes missing a new picture.

Kishore is urging me to write his life story.

'Your life would make a most interesting story,' I tell him. 'But it will be interesting only if I put in everything—your successes *and* your failures.'

'No, no, only successes,' exhorts Kishore. 'I want you to describe me as a popular music director.'

'But you have yet to become popular.'

'I will be popular if you write about me.'

Fortunately we are interrupted by the cots being brought in. Then Bhabiji and Shiv go into a huddle, discussing plans for building an extra room. After all, Kamal may be married soon.

One by one, the children get under their quilts. Popat starts massaging Bhabiji's back. She gives him her favourite blessing: 'God protect you and give you lots of children.' If God listens to all of Bhabiji's prayers and blessings, there will never be a fall in the population.

The lights are off and Bhabiji settles down for the night. She is almost asleep when a small voice pipes up: 'Bhabiji, tell us a story.'

At first Bhabiji pretends not to hear; then, when the request is repeated, she says: 'You'll keep Aunty Shobha awake, and then she'll have an excuse for getting up late in the morning.' But the children know Bhabiji's one great weakness, and they renew their demand.

'Your grandmother is tired,' says Arun. 'Let her sleep.'

But Bhabiji's eyes are open. Her mind is going back over the crowded years, and she remembers something very interesting that happened when her younger brother's wife's sister married the eldest son of her third cousin…

Before long, the children are asleep, and I am wondering if I will ever sleep, for Bhabiji's voice drones on, into the darker reaches of the night.

CHACHI'S FUNERAL

Chachi died at 6 p.m. on Wednesday, 5 April, and came to life again exactly twenty minutes later. This is how it happened.

Chachi was, as a rule, a fairly tolerant, easy-going person, who waddled about the house without paying much attention to the swarms of small sons, daughters, nephews and nieces who poured in and out of the rooms. But she had taken a particular aversion to her ten-year-old nephew, Sunil. She was a simple woman and could not understand Sunil. He was a little brighter than her own sons, more sensitive, and inclined to resent a scolding or a cuff across the head. He was better looking than her own children. All this, in addition to the fact that she resented having to cook for the boy while both his parents went out at office jobs, led her to grumble at him a little more than was really necessary.

Sunil sensed his aunt's jealousy and fanned its flames. He was a mischievous boy, and did little things to annoy her, like bursting paper-bags behind her while she dozed, or commenting on the width of her pyjamas when they were hung out to dry. On the evening of 5 April, he had been in particularly high spirits, and feeling hungry, entered the kitchen with the intention of helping himself to some honey. But the honey was on the top shelf, and Sunil wasn't quite tall enough to grasp the bottle. He got his fingers to it but as he tilted it towards him, it fell to the ground with a crash.

Chachi reached the scene of the accident before Sunil could slip away. Removing her slipper, she dealt him three or four furious blows across the head and shoulders. This done, she sat down on the floor and burst into tears.

Had the beating come from someone else, Sunil might have cried; but his pride was hurt, and instead of weeping, he muttered something under his breath and stormed out of the room.

Climbing the steps to the roof, he went to his secret hiding-place, a small hole in the wall of the unused barsati, where he kept his marbles, kite-string, tops and a clasp-knife. Opening the knife, he plunged it thrice into the soft wood of the window-frame.

'I'll kill her!' he whispered fiercely, 'I'll kill her, I'll kill her!'

'Who are you going to kill, Sunil?'

It was his cousin Madhu, a dark, slim girl of twelve, who aided and abetted him in most of his exploits. Sunil's Chachi was her 'Mammi'. It was a very big family.

'Chachi,' said Sunil. 'She hates me, I know. Well, I hate her too. This time I'll kill her.'

'How are you going to do it?'

'I'll stab with this.' He showed her the knife.

'Three times, in the heart.'

'But you'll be caught. The C.I.D. are very clever. Do you want to go to jail?'

'Won't they hang me?'

'They don't hang small boys. They send them to boarding-schools.'

'I don't want to go to a boarding-school.'

'Then better not kill your Chachi. At least not this way. I'll show you how.'

Madhu produced pencil and paper, went down on her hands and knees, and screwing up her face in sharp concentration, made a rough drawing of Chachi. Then, with a red crayon, she sketched in a big heart in the region of Chachi's stomach.

'Now,' she said, 'stab her to death!'

Sunil's eyes shone with excitement. Here was a great new game. You could always depend on Madhu for something original. He held the drawing against the woodwork, and plunged his knife three times into Chachi's pastel breast.

'You have killed her,' said Madhu.

'Is that all?'

'Well, if you like, we can cremate her.'

'All right.'

She took the torn paper, crumpled it up, produced a box of matches from Sunil's hiding-place, lit a match, and set fire to the paper. In a few minutes all that remained of Chachi were a few ashes.

'Poor Chachi,' said Madhu.

'Perhaps we shouldn't have done it,' said Sunil beginning to feel sorry.

'I know, we'll put her ashes in the river!'
'What river?'
'Oh, the drain will do.'

Madhu gathered the ashes together, and leant over the balcony of the roof. She threw out her arms, and the ashes drifted downwards.

Some of them settled on the pomegranate tree, a few reached the drain and were carried away by a sudden rush of kitchen-water. She turned to face Sunil.

Big tears were rolling down Sunil's cheeks.

'What are you crying for?' asked Madhu.

'Chachi. I didn't hate her so much.'

'Then why did you want to kill her?'

'Oh, that was different.'

'Come on, then, let's go down. I have to do my homework.' As they came down the steps from the roof, Chachi emerged from the kitchen.

'Oh Chachi!' shouted Sunil. He rushed to her and tried to get his arms around her ample waist.

'Now what's up?' grumbled Chachi. 'What is it this time?'

'Nothing, Chachi. I love you so much. Please don't leave us.'

A look of suspicion crossed Chachi's face. She frowned down at the boy. But she was reassured by the look of genuine affection that she saw in his eyes.

'Perhaps he *does* care for me, after all,' she thought and patting him gently on the head, she took him by the hand and led him back to the kitchen.

THE LAST TIME I SAW DELHI

I'd had this old and faded negative with me for a number of years and had never bothered to make a print from it. It was a picture of my maternal grandparents. I remembered my grandmother quite well, because a large part of my childhood had been spent in her house in Dehra after she had been widowed; but although everyone said she was fond of me, I remembered her as a stern, somewhat aloof person, of whom I was a little afraid.

I hadn't kept many family pictures and this negative was yellow and spotted with damp.

Then last week, when I was visiting my mother in hospital in Delhi, while she awaited her operation, we got talking about my grandparents, and I remembered the negative and decided I'd make a print for my mother.

When I got the photograph and saw my grandmother's face for the first time in twenty-five years, I was immediately struck by my resemblance to her. I have, like her, lived a rather spartan life, happy with my one room, just as she was content to live in a room of her own while the rest of the family took over the house! And like her, I have lived tidily. But I did not know the physical resemblance was so close—the fair hair, the heavy build, the wide forehead. She looks more like me than my mother!

In the photograph she is seated on her favourite chair, at the top of the veranda steps, and Grandfather stands behind her in the shadows thrown by a large mango tree which is not in the picture. I can tell it was a mango tree because of the pattern the leaves make on the wall. Grandfather was a slim, trim man, with a drooping moustache that was fashionable in the 1920s. By all accounts he had a mischievous sense of humour, although he looks unwell in the picture. He appears to have been quite swarthy. No wonder he was so successful in dressing up 'native' style and passing himself off as a street vendor. My mother tells me he even took my grandmother in on one occasion, and sold her a basketful of bad oranges. His character was in strong contrast to my grandmother's rather forbidding personality and Victorian sense of propriety; but they made a good match.

So here's the picture, and I am taking it to show my mother who lies in the Lady Hardinge Hospital, awaiting the removal of her left breast.

It is early August and the day is hot and sultry. It rained during the night, but now the sun is out and the sweat oozes through my shirt as I sit in the back of a stuffy little taxi taking me through the suburbs of Greater New Delhi.

On either side of the road are the houses of well-to-do Punjabis who came to Delhi as refugees in 1947 and now make up more than half the capital's population. Industrious, flashy, go-ahead people. Thirty years ago, fields extended on either side of this road as far as the eye could see. The Ridge, an outcrop of the Aravallis, was scrub jungle, in which the black buck roamed. Feroz Shah's fourteenth century hunting lodge stood here in splendid isolation. It is still here, hidden by petrol pumps and lost in the sounds of buses, cars, trucks and scooter rickshaws. The peacock has fled the forest, the black buck is extinct. Only the jackal remains. When, a thousand years from now, the last human has left this contaminated planet for some other star, the jackal and the crow will remain, to survive for years on all the refuse we leave behind.

It is difficult to find the right entrance to the hospital, because for about a mile along the Panchkuian Road the pavement has been obliterated by tea shops, furniture shops, and piles of accumulated junk. A public hydrant stands near the gate, and dirty water runs across the road.

I find my mother in a small ward. It is a cool, dark room, and a ceiling fan whirrs pleasantly overhead. A nurse, a dark, pretty girl from the South, is attending to my mother. She says, 'In a minute,' and proceeds to make an entry on a chart.

My mother gives me a wan smile and beckons me to come nearer. Her cheeks are slightly flushed, due possibly to fever, otherwise she looks her normal self. I find it hard to believe that the operation she will have tomorrow will only give her, at the most, another year's lease on life.

I sit at the foot of her bed. This is my third visit since I flew back from Jersey, using up all my savings in the process; and I will leave after the operation, not to fly away again, but to return to the hills which have always called me back.

'How do you feel?' I ask.

'All right. They say they will operate in the morning. They've stopped my smoking.'

'Can you drink? Your rum, I mean?'

'No. Not until a few days after the operation.'

She has a fair amount of grey in her hair, natural enough at fifty-four. Otherwise she hasn't changed much; the same small chin and mouth, lively brown eyes. Her father's face, not her mother's.

The nurse has left us. I produce the photograph and hand it to my mother.

'The negative was lying with me all these years. I had it printed yesterday.'

'I can't see without my glasses.'

The glasses are lying on the locker near her bed. I hand them to her. She puts them on and studies the photograph.

'Your grandmother was always very fond of you.'

'It was hard to tell. She wasn't a soft woman.'

'It was her money that got you to Jersey, when you finished school. It wasn't much, just enough for the ticket.'

'I didn't know that.'

'The only person who ever left you anything. I'm afraid I've nothing to leave you, either.'

'You know very well that I've never cared a damn about money. My father taught me to write. That was inheritance enough.'

'And what did I teach you?'

'I'm not sure... Perhaps you taught me how to enjoy myself now and then.'

She looked pleased at this. 'Yes, I've enjoyed myself

between troubles. But your father didn't know how to enjoy himself. That's why we quarrelled so much. And finally separated.'

'He was much older than you.'

'You've always blamed me for leaving him, haven't you?'

'I was very small at the time. You left us suddenly. My father had to look after me, and it wasn't easy for him. He was very sick. Naturally, I blamed you.'

'He wouldn't let me take you away.'

'Because you were going to marry someone else.'

I break off; we have been over this before. I am not here as my father's advocate, and the time for recrimination has passed.

And now it is raining outside, and the scent of wet earth comes through the open doors, overpowering the odour of medicines and disinfectants. The dark-eyed nurse comes in again and informs me that the doctor will soon be on his rounds. I can come again in the evening or early morning before the operation.

'Come in the evening,' says my mother. 'The others will be here then.'

'I haven't come to see the others.'

'They are looking forward to seeing you.' 'They' being my stepfather and half-brothers.

'I'll be seeing them in the morning.'

'As you like…'

And then I am on the road again, standing on the pavement, on the fringe of a chaotic rush of traffic, in which it appears that every vehicle is doing its best to overtake its neighbour. The blare of horns can be heard in the corridors of the hospital, but everyone is conditioned to the noise and pays no attention to it. Rather, the sick and the dying are heartened by the thought that people are still well enough to feel reckless, indifferent to each other's safety! In Delhi, there is a feverish desire to be first in line, the first to get anything... This is probably because no one ever gets round to dealing with second-comers.

When I hail a scooter rickshaw and it stops a short distance away, someone elbows his way past me and gets in first. This epitomizes the philosophy and outlook of the Delhiwallah.

So I stand on the pavement waiting for another scooter, which doesn't come. In Delhi, to be second in the race is to be last.

I walk all the way back to my small hotel, with a foreboding of having seen my mother for the last time.

UNTOUCHABLE

The sweeper boy splashed water over the khus matting that hung in the doorway and for a while the air was cooled.

I sat on the edge of my bed, staring out of the open window, brooding upon the dusty road shimmering in the noonday heat. A car passed and the dust rose in billowing clouds.

Across the road lived the people who were supposed to look after me while my father lay in hospital with malaria. I was supposed to stay with them, sleep with them. But except for meals, I kept away. I did not like them and they did not like me.

For a week, longer probably, I was going to live alone in the red-brick bungalow on the outskirts of the town, on the fringe of the jungle. At night the sweeper boy would keep guard, sleeping in the kitchen. Apart from him, I had no company; only the neighbours' children, and I did not like them and they did not like me.

Their mother said, 'Don't play with the sweeper boy, he is unclean. Don't touch him. Remember, he is a servant. You must come and play with my boys.'

Well, I did not intend playing with the sweeper boy; but neither did I intend playing with her children. I was going to sit on my bed all week and wait for my father to come home.

Sweeper boy...all day he pattered up and down between the house and the water tank, with the bucket clanging against his knees.

Back and forth, with a wide, friendly smile.

I frowned at him.

He was about my age, ten. He had short-cropped hair, very white teeth, and muddy feet, hands and face. All he wore was an old pair of khaki shorts; the rest of his body was bare, burnt a deep brown.

At every trip to the water tank he bathed, and returned dripping and glistening from head to toe.

I dripped with sweat.

It was supposedly below my station to bathe at the tank, where the gardener, water-carrier, cooks, ayahs, sweepers and their children all collected. I was the son of a 'sahib' and convention ruled that I did not play with servant children.

But I was just as determined not to play with the other sahibs' children, for I did not like them and they did not like me.

I watched the flies buzzing against the windowpane, the lizards scuttling across the rafters, the wind scattering petals of scorched, long-dead flowers.

The sweeper boy smiled and saluted in play. I avoided his eyes and said, 'Go away.'

He went into the kitchen.

I rose and crossed the room, and lifted my sun helmet off the hatstand.

A centipede ran down the wall, across the floor.

I screamed and jumped on the bed, shouting for help.

The sweeper boy darted in. He saw me on the bed, the centipede on the floor; and picking a large book off the shelf, slammed it down on the repulsive insect.

I remained standing on my bed, trembling with fear and revulsion.

He laughed at me, showing his teeth, and I blushed and said, 'Get out!'

I would not, could not, touch or approach the hat or hatstand. I sat on the bed and longed for my father to come home.

A mosquito passed close by me and sang in my ear. Half-heartedly, I clutched at it and missed; and it disappeared behind the dressing table.

That mosquito, I reasoned, gave the malaria to my father. And now it was trying to give it to me!

The next-door lady walked through the compound and smiled thinly from outside the window. I glared back at her.

The sweeper boy passed with the bucket and grinned. I turned away.

In bed at night, with the lights on, I tried reading. But even books could not quell my anxiety.

The sweeper boy moved about the house, bolting doors, fastening windows. He asked me if I had any orders.

I shook my head.

He skipped across to the electric switch, turned off the light, and slipped into his quarters. Outside, inside, all was dark; only one shaft of light squeezed in through a crack in the sweeper boy's door, and then that too went out.

I began to wish I had stayed with the neighbours. The darkness worried me—silent and close—silent, as if in suspense.

Once a bat flew flat against the window, falling to the ground outside; once an owl hooted. Sometimes a dog barked. And I tautened as a jackal howled hideously in the jungle behind the bungalow. But nothing could break the overall stillness, the night's silence...

Only a dry puff of wind...

It rustled in the trees, and put me in mind of a snake slithering over dry leaves and twigs. I remembered a tale I had been told not long ago, of a sleeping boy who had been bitten by a cobra.

I would not, could not, sleep. I longed for my father...

The shutters rattled, the doors creaked. It was a night for ghosts.

Ghosts!

God, why did I have to think of them?

My God! There, standing by the bathroom door...

My father! My father dead from the malaria and come to see me!

I threw myself at the switch. The room lit up. I sank down on the bed in complete exhaustion, the sweat soaking my nightclothes.

It was not my father I had seen. It was his dressing gown

hanging on the bathroom door. It had not been taken with him to the hospital.

I turned off the light.

The hush outside seemed deeper, nearer. I remembered the centipede, the bat, thought of the cobra and the sleeping boy; pulled the sheet tight over my head. If I could see nothing, well then, nothing could see me.

A thunderclap shattered the brooding stillness.

A streak of lightning forked across the sky, so close that even through the sheet I saw a tree and the opposite house silhouetted against the flashing canvas of gold.

I dived deeper beneath the bedclothes, gathered the pillow about my ears.

But at the next thunderclap, louder this time, louder than I had ever heard, I leapt from my bed. I could not stand it. I fled, blundering into the sweeper boy's room.

The boy sat on the bare floor.

'What is happening?' he asked.

The lightning flashed, and his teeth and eyes flashed with it. Then he was a blur in the darkness.

'I am afraid,' I said.

I moved towards him and my hand touched a cold shoulder.

'Stay here,' he said. 'I too am afraid.'

I sat down, my back against the wall; beside the untouchable, the outcaste...and the thunder and lightning ceased, and the rain came down, swishing and drumming on the corrugated roof.

'The rainy season has started,' observed the sweeper boy,

turning to me. His smile played with the darkness, and then he laughed. And I laughed too, but feebly.

But I was happy and safe. The scent of the wet earth blew in through the skylight and the rain fell harder.

THE FLUTE PLAYER

Down the main road passed big yellow buses, cars, pony-drawn tongas, motorcycles and bullock carts. This steady flow of traffic seemed, somehow, to form a barrier between the city on one side of the Trunk Road, and the distant sleepy villages on the other. It seemed to cut India in half—the India Kamla knew slightly, and the India she had never seen.

Kamla's grandmother lived on the outskirts of the city of Jaipur, and just across the road from the house there were fields and villages stretching away for hundreds of miles. But Kamla had never been across the main road. This separated the busy city from the flat, green plains stretching endlessly towards the horizon.

Kamla was used to city life. In England, it was London and Manchester. In India, it was Delhi and Jaipur. Rainy Manchester was, of course, different in many ways from sun-drenched Jaipur, and Indian cities had stronger smells and more vibrant colours than their English counterparts. Nevertheless, they had much in common: busy people always on the move, money constantly changing hands, buses to catch, schools to attend, parties to go to, TV to watch. Kamla had seen very little of the English countryside, even less of India outside the cities.

Her parents lived in Manchester where her father was a doctor in a large hospital. She went to school in England. But this year, during the summer holidays, she had come to India to stay with her grandmother. Apart from a maidservant and a grizzled old nightwatchman, Grandmother lived quite alone in a small house on the outskirts of Jaipur. During the winter months, Jaipur's climate was cool and bracing but in the summer, a fierce sun poured down upon the city from a cloudless sky.

None of the other city children ventured across the main road into the fields of millet, wheat and cotton, but Kamla was determined to visit the fields before she returned to England. From the flat roof of the house she could see them stretching away for miles, the ripening wheat swaying in the hot wind. Finally, when there were only two days left before she went to Delhi to board a plane for London, she made up her mind and crossed the main road.

She did this in the afternoon, when Grandmother was asleep and the servants were in the bazaar. She slipped out of the back door and her slippers kicked up the dust as she ran down the path to the main road. A bus roared past and more dust rose from the road and swirled about her. Kamla ran through the dust, past the jacaranda trees that lined the road, and into the fields.

Suddenly, the world became an enormous place, bigger and more varied than it had seemed from the air, also mysterious and exciting—and just a little frightening.

The sea of wheat stretched away till it merged with the hot blinding blue of the sky. Far to her left were a few trees and the low white huts of a village. To her right lay hollow pits of red dust and a blackened chimney where bricks used to be made. In front, some distance away, Kamla could see a camel moving round a well, drawing up water for the fields. She set out in the direction of the camel.

Her grandmother had told her not to wander off on her own in the city; but this wasn't the city, and as far as she knew, camels did not attack people.

It took her a long time to get to the camel. It was about half a mile away, though it seemed much nearer. And when Kamla reached it, she was surprised to find that there was no one else in sight. The camel was turning the wheel by itself, moving round and round the well, while the water kept gushing up in little trays to run down the channels into the fields. The camel took no notice of Kamla, did not look at her even once, just carried on about its business.

There must be someone here, thought Kamla, walking towards a mango tree that grew a few yards away. Ripe mangoes dangled like globules of gold from its branches. Under the tree, fast asleep, was a boy.

All he wore was a pair of dirty white shorts. His body had been burnt dark by the sun; his hair was tousled, his feet chalky with dust. In the palm of his outstretched hand was a flute. He was a thin boy, with long bony legs, but Kamla felt that he was strong too, for his body was hard and wiry.

Kamla came nearer to the sleeping boy, peering at him

with some curiosity, for she had not seen a village boy before. Her shadow fell across his face. The coming of the shadow woke the boy. He opened his eyes and stared at Kamla. When she did not say anything, he sat up, his head a little to one side, his hands clasping his knees, and stared at her.

'Who are you?' he asked a little gruffly. He was not used to waking up and finding strange girls staring at him.

'I'm Kamla. I've come from England, but I'm really from India. I mean I've come home to India, but I'm really from England.' This was going to be rather confusing, so she countered with an abrupt, 'Who are you?'

'I'm the strongest boy in the village,' said the boy, deciding to assert himself without any more ado. 'My name is Romi. I can wrestle and swim and climb any tree.'

'And do you sleep a lot?' asked Kamla innocently.

Romi scratched his head and grinned.

'I must look after the camel,' he said. 'It is no use staying awake for the camel. It keeps going round the well until it is tired, and then it stops. When it has rested, it starts going round again. It can carry on like that all day. But it eats a lot.'

Mention of the camel's food reminded Romi that he was hungry. He was growing fast these days and was nearly always hungry. There were some mangoes lying beside him, and he offered one to Kamla. They were silent for a few minutes. You cannot suck mangoes and talk at the same time. After they had finished, they washed their hands in the water from one of the trays.

'There are parrots in the tree,' said Kamla, noticing three or four green parrots conducting a noisy meeting in the topmost branches. They reminded her a bit of a pop group she had seen and heard at home.

'They spoil most of the mangoes,' said Romi.

He flung a stone at them, missed, but they took off with squawks of protest, flashes of green and gold wheeling in the sunshine.

'Where do you swim?' asked Kamla. 'Down in the well?'

'Of course not. I'm not a frog. There is a canal not far from here. Come, I will show you!'

As they crossed the fields, a pair of blue jays flew out of a bush, rockets of bright blue that dipped and swerved, rising and falling as they chased each other.

Remembering a story that Grandmother had told her, Kamla said, 'They are sacred birds, aren't they? Because of their blue throats.' She told him the story of the God Shiva having a blue throat because he had swallowed a poison that would have destroyed the world; he had kept the poison in his throat and would not let it go further. 'And so his throat is blue, like the blue jay's.'

Romi liked this story. His respect for Kamla greatly increased. But he was not to be outdone, and when a small grey squirrel dashed across the path he told her that squirrels too, were sacred. Krishna, the god who had been born into a farmer's family like Romi's, had been fond of squirrels and would take them in his arms and stroke them. 'That is why squirrels have four dark lines down their backs,' said Romi. 'Krishna was very dark, as dark as I am, and the stripes are the marks of his fingers.'

'Can you catch a squirrel?' asked Kamla.

'No, they are too quick. But I caught a snake once. I caught it by its tail and dropped it in the old well. That well is full of snakes. Whenever we catch one, instead of killing it, we drop it in the well! They can't get out.'

Kamla shuddered at the thought of all those snakes swimming and wriggling about at the bottom of the deep well. She wasn't sure that she wanted to return to the well with him. But she forgot about the snakes when they reached the canal.

It was a small canal, about ten metres wide, and only waist-deep in the middle, but it was very muddy at the bottom. She had never seen such a muddy stream in her life.

'Would you like to get in?' asked Romi.

'No,' said Kamla. 'You get in.'

Romi was only too ready to show off his tricks in the water. His toes took a firm hold on the grassy bank, the muscles of his calves tensed, and he dived into the water with a loud splash, landing rather awkwardly on his belly. It was a poor dive, but Kamla was impressed.

Romi swam across to the opposite bank and then back again. When he climbed out of the water, he was covered with mud. It made him look quite fierce. 'Come on in,' he invited. 'It's not deep.'

'It's dirty,' said Kamla, but felt tempted all the same.

'It's only mud,' said Romi. 'There's nothing wrong with mud. Camels like mud. Buffaloes love mud.'

'I'm not a camel—or a buffalo.'

'All right. You don't have to go right in, just walk along the sides of the channel.'

After a moment's hesitation, Kamla slipped her feet out of her slippers, and crept cautiously down the slope till her feet were in the water. She went no further, but even so, some of the muddy water splashed on to her clean white skirt. What would she tell Grandmother? Her feet sank into the soft mud and she gave a little squeal as the water reached her knees. It was with some difficulty that she got each foot out of the sticky mud.

Romi took her by the hand, and they went stumbling along the side of the channel while little fish swam in and out of their legs, and a heron, one foot raised, waited until they had passed before snapping a fish out of the water. The little fish glistened in the sun before it disappeared down the heron's throat.

Romi gave a sudden exclamation and came to a stop. Kamla held on to him for support.

'What is it?' she asked, a little nervously.

'It's a tortoise,' said Romi. 'Can you see it?'

He pointed to the bank of the canal, and there, lying quite still, was a small tortoise. Romi scrambled up the bank and, before Kamla could stop him, had picked up the tortoise. As soon as he touched it, the animal's head and legs disappeared into its shell. Romi turned it over, but from behind the breastplate only the head and a spiky tail were visible.

'Look!' exclaimed Kamla, pointing to the ground where the tortoise had been lying. 'What's in that hole?'

They peered into the hole. It was about half a metre deep, and at the bottom were five or six white eggs, a little smaller than a hen's eggs.

'Put it back,' said Kamla. 'It was sitting on its eggs.'

Romi shrugged and dropped the tortoise back on its hole. It peeped out from behind its shell, saw the children were still present, and retreated into its shell again.

'I must go,' said Kamla. 'It's getting late. Granny will wonder where I have gone.'

They walked back to the mango tree, and washed their hands and feet in the cool clear water from the well; but only after Romi had assured Kamla that there weren't any snakes in the well—he had been talking about an old disused well on the far side of the village. Kamla told Romi she would take him to her house one day, but it would have to be next year, or perhaps the year after, when she came to India again.

'Is it very far, where you are going?' asked Romi.

'Yes, England is across the seas. I have to go back to my parents. And my school is there, too. But I will take the plane from Delhi. Have you ever been to Delhi?'

'I have not been further than Jaipur,' said Romi. 'What is England like? Are there canals to swim in?'

'You can swim in the sea. Lots of people go swimming in the sea. But it's too cold most of the year. Where I live, there are shops and cinemas and places where you can eat anything you like. And people from all over the world come to live there. You can see red faces, brown faces, black faces, white faces!'

'I saw a red face once,' said Romi. 'He came to the village to take pictures. He took one of me sitting on the camel. He said he would send me the picture, but it never came.'

Kamla noticed the flute lying on the grass. 'Is it your flute?' she asked.

'Yes,' said Romi. 'It is an old flute. But the old ones are best. I found it lying in a field last year. Perhaps it was the God Krishna's! He was always playing the flute.'

'And who taught you to play it?'

'Nobody. I learnt by myself. Shall I play it for you?'

Kamla nodded, and they sat down on the grass, leaning against the trunk of the mango tree, and Romi put the flute to his lips and began to play.

It was a slow, sweet tune, a little sad, a little happy, and the notes were taken up by the breeze and carried across the fields. There was no one to hear the music except the birds and the camel and Kamla. Whether the camel liked it or not, we shall never know; it just kept going round and round the well, drawing up water for the fields. And whether the birds liked it or not, we cannot say, although it is true that they were all suddenly silent when Romi began to play. But Kamla was charmed by the music, and she watched Romi while he played, and the boy smiled at her with his eyes and ran his fingers along the flute. When he stopped playing, everything was still, everything silent, except for the soft wind sighing in the wheat and the gurgle of water coming up from the well.

Kamla stood up to leave.

'When will you come again?' asked Romi.

'I will try to come next year,' said Kamla.

'That is a long time. By then you will be quite old. You may not want to come.'

'I will come,' said Kamla.

'Promise?'

'Promise.'

Romi put the flute in her hands and said, 'You keep it. I can get another one.'

'But I don't know how to play it,' said Kamla.

'It will play by itself,' said Romi.

She took the flute and put it to her lips and blew on it, producing a squeaky little note that startled a lone parrot out of the mango tree. Romi laughed, and while he was laughing, Kamla turned and ran down the path through the fields. And when she had gone some distance, she turned and waved to Romi with the flute. He stood near the well and waved back at her.

Cupping his hands to his mouth, he shouted across the fields, 'Don't forget to come next year!'

And Kamla called back, 'I won't forget.' But her voice was faint, and the breeze blew the words away and Romi did not hear them.

'Was England home?' wondered Kamla. Or was this Indian city home? Or was her true home in that other India, across the busy Trunk Road? Perhaps she would find out one day.

Romi watched her until she was just a speck in the distance, and then he turned and shouted at the cancel, telling it to move faster. But the camel did not even glance at him; it just carried on as before, as India has carried on for thousands of years, round and round and round the well, while the water gurgled and splashed over the smooth stones.

HANGING AT THE MANGO TOPE

The two captive policemen, Inspector Hukam Singh and Sub-Inspector Guler Singh, were being pushed unceremoniously along the dusty, deserted, sun-drenched road. The people of the village had made themselves scarce. They would reappear only when the dacoits went away.

The leader of the dacoit gang was Mangal Singh Bundela, great-grandson of a Pindari adventurer who had been a thorn in the side of the British. Mangal was doing his best to be a thorn in the flesh of his own government. The local police force had been strengthened recently but it was still inadequate for dealing with the dacoits who knew the ravines better than any surveyor. The dacoit Mangal had made a fortune out of ransom. His chief victims were the sons of wealthy industrialists, moneylenders and landowners. But today he had captured two police officials; of no value as far as ransom went, but prestigious prisoners who could be put to other uses...

Mangal Singh wanted to show off in front of the police. He would kill at least one of them—his reputation demanded it but he would let the other go, in order that his legendary power and ruthlessness be given maximum publicity. A legend is always a help!

His red-and-green turban was tied rakishly to one side. His dhoti extended right down to his ankles. His slippers were embroidered with gold and silver thread. His weapon was not ancient matchlock but a well-greased .303 rifle. Two of his men had similar rifles. Some had revolvers. Only the smaller fry carried swords or country-made pistols. Mangal Singh's gang, though traditional in many ways, was up-to-date in the matter of weapons. Right now they had the policemen's guns too.

'Come along, Inspector Sahib,' said Mangal Singh, in tones of polite barbarity, tugging at the rope that encircled the stout Inspector's midriff. 'Had you captured me today, you would have been a hero. You would have taken all the credit even though you could not keep up with your men in the ravines. Too bad you chose to remain sitting in your jeep with the Sub-Inspector. The jeep will be useful to us. You will not. But I would like you to be a hero all the same and there is none better than a dead hero!' Mangal Singh's followers doubled up with laughter. They loved their leader's cruel sense of humour.

'As for you, Guler Singh,' he continued, giving his attention to the Sub-Inspector, 'you are a man from my own village. You should have joined me long ago. But you were never to be trusted. You thought there would be better pickings in the police, didn't you?'

Guler Singh said nothing, simply hung his head and wondered what his fate would be. He felt certain that Mangal

Singh would devise some diabolical and fiendish method of dealing with his captives. Guler Singh's only hope was Constable Ghanshyam, who hadn't been caught by the dacoits because, at the time of the ambush, he had been in the bushes relieving himself.

'To the mango tope,' said Mangal Singh, prodding the policemen forward.

'Listen to me, Mangal,' said the perspiring Inspector, who was ready to try anything to get out of his predicament. 'Let me go and I give you my word there'll be no trouble for you in this area as long as I am posted here. What could be more convenient than that?'

'Nothing,' said Mangal Singh. 'But your word isn't good. My word is different. I have told my men that I will hang you at the mango tope and I mean to keep my word. But I believe in fair play—I like a little sport! You may yet go free if your friend here, Sub-Inspector Guler Singh, has his wits about him.'

The Inspector and his subordinate exchanged doubtful, puzzled looks. They were not to remain puzzled for long. On reaching the mango tope, the dacoits produced a good strong hempen rope, one end looped into a slip knot. Many a garland of marigolds had the Inspector received during his mediocre career. Now, for the first time, he was being garlanded with a hangman's noose. He had seen hangings, he had rather enjoyed them, but he had no stomach for his own. The Inspector begged for mercy. Who wouldn't have in his position?

'Be quiet,' commanded Mangal Singh. 'I do not want to

know about your wife and your children and the manner in which they will starve. You shot my son last year.'

'Not I!' cried the Inspector. 'It was some other.'

'You led the party. But now, just to show you that I'm a sporting fellow, I am going to have you strung up from this tree and then I am going to give Guler Singh six shots with a rifle, and if he can sever the rope that suspends you before you are dead, well then, you can remain alive and I will let you go! For your sake I hope the Sub-Inspector's aim is good. He will have to shoot fast. My man Phambiri, who has made this noose, was once the executioner in a city jail. He guarantees that you won't last more than fifteen seconds at the end of his rope.'

Guler Singh was taken to a spot about forty yards away. A rifle was thrust into his hands. Two dacoits clambered into the branches of the mango tree. The Inspector, his hands tied behind, could only gaze at them in horror. His mouth opened and shut as though he already had need of more air. And then, suddenly, the rope went taut, up went the Inspector, his throat caught in a vice, while the branch of the tree shook and mango blossoms fluttered to the ground. The Inspector dangled from the rope, his feet about three feet above the ground.

'You can shoot,' said Mangal Singh, nodding to the Sub-Inspector.

And Guler Singh, his hands trembling a little, raised the rifle to his shoulder and fired three shots in rapid succession. But the rope was swinging violently and the Inspector's body was jerking about like a fish on a hook. The bullets went wide.

Guler Singh found the magazine empty. He reloaded, wiped the stinging sweat from his eyes, raised the rifle again, took more careful aim. His hands were steadier now. He rested the sights on the upper portion of the rope, where there was less motion. Normally, he was a good shot but he had never been asked to demonstrate his skill in circumstances such as these.

The Inspector still gyrated at the end of his rope. There was life in him yet. His face was purple. The world, in those choking moments, was a medley of upside-down roofs and a red sun spinning slowly towards him.

Guler Singh's rifle cracked again. An inch or two wide this time. But the fifth shot found its mark, sending small tuffs of rope winging into the air.

The shot did not sever the rope; it was only a nick.

Guler Singh had one shot left. He was quite calm. The rifle sight followed the rope's swing, less agitated now that the Inspector's convulsions were lessening. Guler Singh felt sure he could sever the rope this time.

And then, as his finger touched the trigger, an odd, disturbing thought slipped into his mind, stayed there, throbbing. '*Whose life are you trying to save? Hukam Singh has stood in the way of your promotion more than once. He had you chargesheeted for accepting fifty rupees from an unlicenced rickshaw-puller. He makes you do all the dirty work, blames you when things go wrong, takes the credit when there is credit to be taken. But for him, you'd be an inspector!*'

The rope swayed slightly to the right. The rifle moved just a fraction to the left. The last shot rang out, clipping a sliver of bark from the mango tree.

The Inspector was dead when they cut him down.

'Bad luck,' said Mangal Singh Bundela. 'You nearly saved him. But the next time I catch up with you, Guler Singh, it will be your turn to hang from the mango tree. So keep well away! You know that I am a man of my word. I keep it now by giving you your freedom.'

A few minutes later the party of dacoits had melted away into the late afternoon shadows of the scrub forest. There was the sound of a jeep starting up. Then silence—a silence so profound that it seemed to be shouting in Guler Singh's ears.

As the village people began to trickle out of their houses, Constable Ghanshyam appeared as if from nowhere, swearing that he had lost his way in the jungle. Several people had seen the incident from their windows. They were unanimous in praising the Sub-Inspector for his brave attempt to save his superior's life. He had done his best.

'It is true,' thought Guler Singh. 'I did my best.'

That moment of hesitation before the last shot, the question that had suddenly reared up in the darkness of his mind, had already gone from his memory. We remember only what we want to remember.

'I did my best,' he told everyone.

And so he had.

A MAN CALLED BRAIN

Did Frank Brain possess any redeeming qualities? If so, they were hard to detect. If ever there was a man totally immersed in himself, and in his own sensual pleasures, it was Brain. He had a way with women—spent money on them, seduced them, discarded them—but he had no real friends, just a few layabouts who drank his whisky and listened admiringly to his bragging. And he never stopped bragging.

He bragged about the money he made; he bragged about the influence he had in political circles; he bragged about the socialite women he'd seduced, and the children he had supposedly fathered—although no one had seen any dependants or any indication that he supported them.

Frank Brain supported no one but himself.

And I hated him!

I hated him right from the start—from the time he gave me a bar of chocolate and told me to go out and play in the garden as he had some important business to discuss with my mother. Seven-year-olds are not so easily fooled. I took a round of the garden, ate some of the chocolate, then crept up to the sitting-room window and peered through the glass. Frank Brain had an arm around my mother, and his fat lips pressed against her ear—a business conversation, no doubt.

I rapped loudly on the windowpane, then took off and hid in the shrubbery. The front door opened, and Frank Brain stepped out on the veranda, cursing loudly. A cat was sleeping on the doormat. He kicked it away, then drew back and closed the door. I waited a few minutes, then threw a pebble at the front door. Out came Brain again, using all the foul language that made up most of his limited vocabulary. The cat streaked across the lawn, in search of sanctuary.

Presently Frank Brain got into his car and drove away. It was a World War II Packard, big and showy like its owner, but heavy on petrol.

Frank Brain was a frequent visitor to the house in Dehra, where my mother and I were staying while my father was on active RAF duty, being moved around from Delhi to Karachi to Calcutta to Ceylon.

'Mum, why does Mr Brain keep coming to see us?' I asked one day.

'Why, don't you like him?'

'No. He's fat and ugly and he doesn't stop smoking those smelly cigars.'

'He's been very helpful. And he keeps bringing you presents.'

'I don't want them. When will Daddy come home?'

'When the war's over, I suppose. He may be in Delhi next month. Frank has offered to drive us to Delhi. Won't that be nice?'

'Can't we go on our own? There's a train to Delhi, isn't there?'

'We'll see when the time comes.'

In the meantime, Frank Brain's visits became more frequent. He sold cars on behalf of an American company based in Delhi, but he had a branch office in Dehra and a wife in Clement Town. Brain never invited us to his home, so we never saw the wife, but my mother said she ran a school of her own. And I would soon be sent to a boarding school in the hills, she told me.

∽

The journey to Delhi was a memorable one—one of my earliest memories, in fact—and seventy-five years later I can still recall that drive through the extensive forests of the Doon, through the pass in the Shivalik range, and along the banks of the Ganges canal. Mr Brain at the wheel of his Packard, full of confidence as usual, talking of tigers he had shot and great people he had met; my mother sitting beside him, smoking her favourite Gold Flake from a round tin. And there was I in the back seat, looking at the scenery and only half listening to the one-sided conversation.

'Look, there's a spotted deer!' I exclaimed, as we passed a startled cheetal. But Frank Brain did not slow down; he had time only for tigers.

There wasn't much traffic on the roads in those far-off days; mostly bullock carts and pony-drawn ekkas or tongas. Only a few people possessed motorcars.

We stopped at a canal rest house for a late afternoon

lunch, and then my mother and Mr Brain decided to spend the night there. It was a quiet place, very restful, with only the chowkidar and a couple of village dogs in attendance. Brain had brought his icebox and whisky along, and as the sun went down the soda-water bottles popped and the whisky began to flow... I wandered off on my own, strolling down the path along the canal bank, watching the water move gently, caressingly, downstream. Tall bushes grew along the banks. Parrots flew out of a mango tree. At the bottom of a flight of steps a dhobi was washing clothes, pounding them against the flat stones in what appeared to be an attempt to tear them to pieces.

When I returned to the rest house it was getting dark. The whisky bottle was half empty.

'Where have you been?' asked my mother.

'Just wandering around.'

'Well, your dinner is ready whenever you want it. And then go to bed early. We'll leave before it gets too hot.'

My bed was placed in the middle of a large hall full of connecting doors. Mr Brain and my mother had the bedroom to themselves. Brain had very thoughtfully given me a comic to read. It was called *The Dandy* and I finished it in ten minutes.

My mother came in and bolted all the doors and switched off the light.

'It's lonely in here,' I said.

'It's quite safe. The chowkidar sleeps in the veranda. If you need anything, call for me.'

I tried to sleep but I could hear Frank Brain and my

mother talking in the next room. Apparently another bottle had been opened.

I called out, and Frank Brain opened the door, his huge frame silhouetted against the bedroom light.

'What is it?' he asked.

'Water,' I said. 'I'm thirsty.'

My mother brought me a glass of water.

'Now go to sleep,' she said.

But how do you force yourself to sleep?

I could hear my mother laughing, Frank Brain singing like a drunken sailor, the chowkidar coughing in the veranda, and jackals howling outside the window.

I called out for my mother.

Frank Brain appeared. 'Why don't you go to sleep?'

'I'm thirsty,' I said, 'More water.'

They brought me more water, an entire jugful.

'Now go to sleep,' said Brain, 'or I'll give you a hiding.'

My temper flared up. 'Try giving me a hiding, and I'll *kill* you!'

Frank Brain was shocked into silence. My mother said, 'Don't talk like that!' Brain threw up his arms, cursed in Hindustani (English being inadequate), and stomped out of the room.

And finally, helped by a frog croaking in the bathroom, I fell asleep.

∽

I was reunited with my father in Delhi, and was to live with him for a couple of years, in air force hutments or rented rooms. He wasn't supposed to have a child with him, but somehow he got away with it on compassionate grounds.

My mother came and went occasionally, and finally my parents were legally separated. When my father was transferred to another outpost, I was finally admitted to a boarding school in the hills.

It was many years before I saw Frank Brain again. My father had died, my mother had married a small-town businessman, and I was working in Delhi for a newspaper. On a visit to my mother's, Frank Brain's name cropped up. A visitor, an old friend of my mother's, turned out to be one of Brain's ex-wives or ex-mistresses. She complained bitterly that he had left her stranded with a growing daughter, vehemently denying that she was his child. Apparently, he was now living with a woman he had picked up in a sleazy hotel in the old city.

Always intrigued by someone else's scandals, my mother decided to look him up. For me, he was an unpleasant but distant memory, and I had no wish to see him again, but she phoned him to say she was coming over, and she succeeded in dragging me along.

He was living in a bungalow in a rather nondescript part of West Patel Nagar. It was just off the main road, and a constant stream of traffic thundered past the gate.

Brain had, of course, aged in the twenty years since I had last seen him. His belly sagged over his belt; his chin sagged over his collar; he was almost bald.

But otherwise he was full of his usual bluster and false bonhomie; he hugged my mother, kissed her, shook my hand

and ushered me into his large bed-sitting room where his current mistress was reclining against a pile of pillows at the head of a large double bed.

She was a sex worker from a notorious area in the old city. Her name was Khushboo, and she certainly lived up to her name, for the room was filled with the strong fragrance of jasmine, attar of roses and a host of other perfumes. There was nothing passive about this lady. She appeared to have Frank Brain well under her thumb, or rather under her generous bosom, which was where he spent most of the time. Quite unabashed, she laughed and joked and teased the ageing roué, stroking his wobbly chin and chiding him about his declining sexual powers.

'I have to wait until five in the morning,' she said with a laugh, 'before I can get him to do anything!'

I felt quite embarrassed in this company, but Frank Brain did not seem to mind, and my mother seemed to find it amusing. He was quite smitten with his new companion, and was constantly cuddling her, his hands never still as they roamed over her sensuous body. He was going to marry her, he proclaimed; but we'd heard that before. Frank Brain's affairs and infatuations had never lasted very long; but he was certainly putty in the hands of this queen of her profession. And she seemed quite fond of him, in a bantering sort of way.

But of course she cleaned him out.

∽

It must have been about a year later, when I was passing that way, I stopped outside the gate of Frank Brain's house, wondering if he still lived there. I had no particular desire to see him again, but I was curious... The lights were out and the place looked unoccupied. There was a lock on the front door. It looked as though he had gone away.

I was about to walk on when a man appeared at the next-door gate. 'Are you looking for someone?' he asked.

'Mr Brain,' I said. 'Has he gone away?'

'Died last month. I'm the landlord. Are you a relative?'

I was surprised but not shocked. Frank Brain had led a life of self-indulgence.

'Just an acquaintance,' I said, 'How did he die?'

'Must have been a heart attack. He'd been on his own for several months, no one to look after him when he fell ill.'

'What about the lady who was staying with him?'

'Left long ago. Took away all his furniture and carpets. I suppose he owed her money.'

'Was anyone informed when he died?'

'There was no one to inform. He'd been dead two or three days when we found him. Had to break into the house. Informed the police. They went through his things but couldn't find any addresses or phone numbers. So he was taken to the morgue. Kept there for some time. Unclaimed body.'

'So they had him cremated, I suppose.'

'No. Sent the body to the local medical college. The medical students need bodies for study and dissection. Bodies are in short supply. They take what they can get—usually beggars and vagrants.'

Frank Brain a vagrant! It was an interesting thought. And

by becoming a subject for dissection he had perhaps finally contributed something to society. Perhaps an examination of his brain would reveal something that would account for the vagaries of human nature; but I doubted it.

As I walked away from that empty, denuded house, the words of a childhood poem, 'The Miller of Dee', ran through my head:

> *I care for nobody,*
> *No, not I,*
> *And nobody cares for me.*

And that just about summed up Mr Frank Brain.

SUSANNA'S SEVEN HUSBANDS

Locally, the tomb was known as 'the grave of the seven-times married one'.

You'd be forgiven for thinking it was Bluebeard's grave; he was reputed to have killed several wives in turn because they showed undue curiosity about a locked room. But this was the tomb of Susanna Anna-Maria Yeates, and the inscription (most of it in Latin) stated that she was mourned by all who had benefited from her generosity, her beneficiaries having included various schools, orphanages and the church across the road. There was no sign of any other graves in the vicinity, and presumably her husbands had been interred in the old Rajpur graveyard, below the Delhi Ridge.

I was still in my teens when I first saw the ruins of what had once been a spacious and handsome mansion. Desolate and silent, its well-laid paths were overgrown with weeds, its flower-beds had disappeared under a growth of thorny jungle. The two-storeyed house had looked across the Grand Trunk Road. Now abandoned, feared and shunned, it stood encircled in mystery, reputedly the home of evil spirits.

Outside the gate, along the Grand Trunk Road, thousands

of vehicles sped by—cars, trucks, buses, tractors, bullock-carts—but few noticed the old mansion or its mausoleum, set back as they were from the main road, hidden by mango, neem and peepul trees. One old and massive peepul tree grew out of the ruins of the house, strangling it much as its owner was said to have strangled one of her dispensable paramours.

As a much-married person with a quaint habit of disposing of her husbands whenever she tired of them, Susanna's malignant spirit was said to haunt the deserted garden. I had examined the tomb, I had gazed upon the ruins, I had scrambled through shrubbery and overgrown rose-bushes, but I had not encountered the spirit of this mysterious woman. Perhaps, at the time, I was too pure and innocent to be targeted by malignant spirits. For, malignant she must have been, if the stories about her were true.

No one had been down into the vaults of the ruined mansion. They were said to be occupied by a family of cobras, traditional guardians of buried treasure. Had she really been a woman of great wealth, and could treasure still be buried there? I put these questions to Naushad, the furniture-maker, who had lived in the vicinity all his life, and whose father had made the furniture and fittings for this and other great houses in Old Delhi.

'Lady Susanna, as she was known, was much sought after for her wealth,' recalled Naushad. She was no miser, either. She spent freely, reigning in state in her palatial home, with many horses and carriages at her disposal. You see the stables there, behind the ruins? Now, they are occupied by bats and jackals. Every evening she rode through the Roshanara Gardens, the cynosure of all eyes, for she was beautiful as well as wealthy. Yes, all men sought her favours, and she could choose from the best of them. Many were fortune-hunters. She did not discourage them. Some found favour for a time, but she soon tired of them. None of her husbands enjoyed her wealth for very long!

'Today, no one enters those ruins, where once there was mirth and laughter. She was the zamindari lady, the owner of much land, and she administered her estate with a strong hand. She was kind if rents were paid when they fell due, but terrible if someone failed to pay.'

'Well, over fifty years have gone by since she was laid to rest, but still men speak of her with awe. Her spirit is restless, and it is said that she often visits the scenes of her former splendour. She has been seen walking through this gate, or riding in the gardens or driving in her phaeton down the Rajpur road.'

'And, what happened to all those husbands?' I asked.

'Most of them died mysterious deaths. Even the doctors were baffled. Tomkins Sahib drank too much. The lady soon tired of him. A drunken husband is a burdensome creature, she was heard to say. He would have drunk himself to death, but she was an impatient woman and was anxious to replace him. You see those datura bushes growing wild in the grounds? They have always done well here.'

'Belladonna?' I suggested.

'That's right, huzoor. Introduced in the whisky-soda, they put him to sleep for ever.'

'She was quite humane in her way.'

'Oh, very humane, sir. She hated to see anyone suffer. One sahib, I don't know his name, drowned in the tank behind the house, where the water-lilies grew. But she made sure he was half-dead before he fell in. She had large, powerful hands, they said.'

'Why did she bother to marry them? Couldn't she just have had men friends?'

'Not in those days, dear sir. Respectable society would not have tolerated it. Neither in India nor in the West would it have been permitted.'

'She was born out of her time,' I remarked.

'True, sir. And remember, most of them were fortune-hunters. So, we need not waste too much pity on them.'

'*She* did not waste any.'

'She was without pity. Especially when she found out what they were really after. The snakes had a better chance of survival.'

'How did the other husbands take their leave of this world?'

'Well, the Colonel-sahib shot himself while cleaning his rifle. Purely an accident, huzoor. Although some say she had loaded his gun without his knowledge. Such was her reputation by now that she was suspected even when innocent. But she bought her way out of trouble. It was easy enough, if you were wealthy.'

'And, the fourth husband?'

'Oh, he died a natural death. There was a cholera epidemic that year, and he was carried off by the haija.

Although, again, there were some who said that a good dose of arsenic produced the same symptoms! Anyway, it was cholera on the death certificate. And, the doctor who signed it was the next to marry her.'

'Being a doctor, he was probably quite careful about what he ate and drank.

'He lasted about a year.'

'What happened?'

'He was bitten by a cobra.'

'Well, that was just bad luck, wasn't it? You could hardly blame it on Susanna.'

'No, huzoor, but the cobra was in his bedroom. It was coiled around the bed-post. And, when he undressed for the night, it struck! He was dead when Susanna came into the room an hour later. She had a way with snakes. She did not harm them and they never attacked her.'

'And, there were no antidotes in those days. Exit the doctor. Who was the sixth husband?'

'A handsome man. An indigo planter. He had gone bankrupt when the indigo trade came to an end. He was hoping to recover his fortune with the good lady's help. But our Susanna-mem, she did not believe in sharing her fortune with anyone.'

'How did she remove the indigo planter?'

'It was said that she lavished strong drink upon him, and when he lay helpless, she assisted him on the road we all have to take by pouring molten lead in his ears.'

'A painless death, I'm told.'

'But a terrible price to pay huzoor, simply because one

is no longer needed....'

We walked along the dusty highway, enjoying the evening breeze, and some time later we entered the Roshanara Gardens, in those days Delhi's most popular and fashionable meeting place.

'You have told me how six of her husbands died, Naushad. I thought there were seven?'

'Ah, a gallant young magistrate, who perished right here, huzoor. They were driving through the park after dark when the lady's carriage was attacked by brigands. In defending her, the gallant young man received a fatal sword wound.'

'Not the lady's fault, Naushad.'

'No, my friend. But he was a magistrate, remember, and the assailants, one of whose relatives had been convicted by him, were out for revenge. Oddly enough, though, two of the men were given employment by the lady Susanna at a later date. You may draw your own conclusions.'

'And, were there others?'

'Not husbands. But an adventurer, a soldier of fortune came along. He found her treasure, they say. He lies buried with it, in the cellars of the ruined house. His bones lie scattered there, among gold and silver and precious jewels. The cobras guard them still! But how he perished was a mystery, and remains so till this day.'

'What happened to Susanna?'

'She lived to a good old age, as you know. If she paid for her crimes, it wasn't in this life! As you know, she had no children. But she started an orphanage and gave generously to the poor and to various schools and institutions, including a home for widows. She died peacefully in her sleep.'

'A merry widow,' I remarked. 'The Black Widow spider!'

Don't go looking for Susanna's tomb. It vanished some years ago, along with the ruins of her mansion. A smart new housing estate came up on the site, but not after several workmen and a contractor succumbed to snake bite! Occasionally, residents complain of a malignant ghost in their midst, who is given to flagging down cars, especially those driven by single men. There have been one or two mysterious disappearances. Ask anyone living along this stretch of the Delhi Ridge, and they'll tell you that's it's true.

And, after dusk, an old-fashioned horse and carriage can sometimes be seen driving through the Roshanara Gardens. Ignore it, my friend. Don't stop to answer any questions from the beautiful fair lady who smiles at you from behind lace curtains. She's still looking for a suitable husband.

STREET OF THE RED WELL

The sun beats down on the sweltering city of Old Delhi. Not a breath of air stirs in the narrow, winding streets. This old Walled City, now over three hundred years old, has no open spaces, no sidewalks, no shady avenues. During the reign of Emperor Shah Jahan, a canal ran down the centre of the main thoroughfare, Chandni Chowk (street of the silversmiths), but the canal has long since been covered over, and the Yamuna river, from which water has been channelled, lies beyond the emperor's fort, the Red Fort of Delhi, where the Prime Minister speaks to the multitude every year on Independence Day.

It is not water that I seek most, but shelter from the heat and glare of the overhead sun. I have chosen what is quite possibly the hottest day in May, the temperature over 105 degrees Fahrenheit, to go walking in search of—what? A story, perhaps, and adventure. Or that is what I set out to do. The heat of the day has willed otherwise. I may be ready for an adventure, but no one else is interested. I am the only one walking the streets from choice.

Shopkeepers nod drowsily beneath whirring ceiling-fans. The pavement barber has taken his customer into the shelter of an awning. A fortune-teller has decided that there is nothing to predict and has fallen asleep under the same awning. A vegetable seller sprinkles water on his vegetables in a dispirited fashion. Those cauliflowers were fresh an hour ago: they look old already. Even the flies are drowsy. Instead of buzzing feverishly from place to place, they stagger about on tired legs.

It is the pigeons who have found all the coolest places. These birds have made the old city their own. New Delhi is for the crows who like to have a tree to sleep in, even if they take their meals from out of kitchens and verandahs. But the pigeons prefer buildings, and the older the buildings the better. They are familiar with every cool alcove or shady recess in the crumbling walls of neglected mosques and mansions.

A fat, supercilious pigeon watches me from the window ledge above a jeweller's shop. The pigeon's forebears settled here long before the British thought of taking Delhi. Conquerors have come and gone, Nadir Shah the Persian, Madhav Rao the Maratha, Gulam Kadir the Rohilla and generations of goldsmiths and silversmiths. Hindus and Muslims have made and lost fortunes in the city, but nothing has disturbed the tranquil life of these pigeons. Their gentle cooing can always be heard when there is a lull in the jagged symphony of traffic noise. How do they manage to sound so cool?

But here's welcome relief for humans; a shady corner in Lai Kuan bazaar (street of the Red Well), where an old man provides drinking water to thirsty wayfarers such as myself. His water is stored in a surahi, an earthenware jug which keeps the water sweet and cool. I bend down, cup my hands, and receive the sparkling liquid as my benefactor tilts the surahi towards me.

Lai Kuan. The Red Well. Of course it is no longer here, but the street still bears its name. And I like to think that here, in the middle of the street, where a bullock has gone to sleep, forcing the cyclists to make a detour, there was once a well, made of dark red brick, where the water bubbled forth all day. Imprisoned beneath the soil, held down by the crowded commercial houses of this old quarter, the water must still be there; it gives nourishment to an old peepul tree that grows beside a temple. It is the only tree in the street. It juts out from the temple wall growing straight and tall, dwarfing the two-storeyed houses. One of its roots, breaking throughout the ground, has curled up to provide a smooth, well-worn seat. And it is cool here, beneath the peepul.

On the other side of the road, a tall iron doorway is set in a high wall. Doors like this were only built in the previous century, when a wealthy merchant's house had to be a miniature fortress as well as a residence. I cannot see over the wall and I would like to know what lies behind the door. Perhaps a side street, perhaps a market, perhaps a garden, perhaps....

The door opens, not easily, because it had been left closed for a long time, but slowly and with much complaint. And beyond the door there is only an empty courtyard, covered with rubble, the ruins of the old house. I am about to turn away when I hear a deep tremendous murmur.

It is the cooing of many pigeons. But where are they?

I advance further into the ruin, and there, opening out in front of me, ready to receive me as the rabbit-hole was ready to receive Alice, is an old, disused well. I peer down into its murky depths. It is dark, very dark down there; but that is where the pigeons live, in the walls of this lost, long-forgotten well shut away from the rest of the city. I cannot see any water, so I drop a pebble over the side. It strikes the wall, and then, with a soft plop, touches water. At that instant there is a rush of air and a tremendous beating of wings, and a flock of pigeons. Thirty or forty of them fly out of the well, streak upwards, circle the building, and then falling into formation, wheel overhead, the sun gleaming white on their underwings.

I have discovered their secret. Now I know why they look so cool, so refreshed, while we who walk the streets of Old Delhi do so with parched mouths and drooping limbs. The pigeons are the only ones who still know about the Red Well.

FOOTLOOSE IN AGRA

I went to Agra in 1965, to see the Taj. But what interested me about the city had little to do with Emperor Shah Jahan's grand monument to his love.

The cycle rickshaw is the best way of getting about Agra. Its smooth gliding motion and leisurely rate of progress are in keeping with the pace of life in this old-world city. The rickshaw boy makes his way through the crowded bazaars, exchanging insults with tonga drivers, pedestrians and other cyclists; but once on the broad Mall or Taj Road, his curses change to carefree song and he freewheels along the tree-lined avenues. Old colonial-style bungalows still stand in large compounds shaded by peepul, banyan, neem and jamun trees.

Looking up, I notice a number of bright paper kites that flutter, dip and swerve in the cloudless sky. I cannot recall seeing so many kites before.

'Is it a festival today?' I ask,

'No, sahib,' says the rickshaw boy. 'Not even a holiday.'

'Then why so many kites?'

He does not even bother to look up. 'You can see kites every day, sahib.'

'I don't see them in Delhi.'

'Ah, but Delhi is a busy place. In Agra, people still fly kites. There are kite-flying competitions every Sunday, and heavy bets are sometimes placed on the outcome.'

As we near the city, I notice kites stuck in trees or dangling from electric wires; but there are always others soaring up to take their place. I ask the rickshaw boy to tell me something about the kite-fliers and the kitemakers, but the subject bores him.

'You had better see the Taj today, sahib.'

'All right take me to it. I can lunch afterwards.'

It is difficult to view the Taj at noon. The sun strikes the white marble, and there is a great dazzle of reflected light. I stand there with averted eyes, looking at everything—the formal gardens, the surrounding walls of red sandstone, the winding river—everything except the monument I have come to see.

It is there, of course, very solid and real, perfectly preserved, with every jade, jasper or lapis lazuli playing its part in the overall design; and after a while, I can shade my eyes and take in a vision of shimmering white marble. The light rises in waves from the paving-stones, and the squares of black and white marble create an effect of running water. Inside the chamber it is cool and dark but rather musty, and I waste no time in hurrying out again into the sunlight.

I walk the length of a gallery and turn with some relief to the river scene. The sluggish Yamuna winds past Agra on its way to its union with the Ganga. I know the Yamuna well. I know it where it emerges from the foothills near Kalsi, cold and blue from the melting snows; I know it as it winds through fields of wheat and sugarcane and mustard, across the flat plains of Uttar Pradesh, sometimes placid, sometimes in flood. I know the river at Delhi, where its muddy banks are a patchwork of clothes spread out by the hundreds of washermen who serve the city and I know it at Mathura, where it is alive with huge turtles; Mathura, sacred city, whose beginnings are lost in antiquity.

And then the river winds its way to Agra, to this spot by the Taj, where parrots flash in the sunshine, kingfishers swoop low over the water and a proud peacock struts across the lawns surrounding the monument.

I follow the peacock into a shady grove. It is quite tame and does not fly away. It leads me to a small boy who is sitting in the shade of a tree, feasting on a handful of small green fruit.

I have not seen the fruit before, and I ask the boy to tell me what it is. He offers me what looks like a hard green plum.

'It is the fruit from the Ashok tree,' says the boy. 'There are many such trees in the garden.'

'Are you allowed to take the fruit?'

'I am allowed,' he says, grinning. 'My father is the head gardener.' I bite into the fruit. It is hard and sour but not unpleasant.

'Do you live here?' I ask.

'Over the wall,' he says. 'But I come here everyday, to help my father and to eat the fruit.'

'So you see the Taj Mahal every day?'

'I have seen it every day for as long as I can remember.'

'And I am seeing it for the first time...you're very lucky.'

He shrugs. 'If you see it once, or a hundred times, it is the same. It doesn't change.'

'Don't you like looking at it, then?'

'I like looking at the people who come here. They are always different. In the evening there will be many people.'

'You must have seen people from almost every country in the world.'

'That is so. They all come here to look at the Taj. Kings and Queens and Presidents and Prime Ministers and film stars and poor people too. And I look at them. In that way it isn't boring.'

'Well, you have the Taj to thank for that.'

He gazes thoughtfully at the shimmering monument.

His eyes are accustomed to the sharp sunlight. He sees the Taj every day, but at this moment he is really looking at it, thinking about it, wondering what magic it must possess to attract people from all corners of the earth, to bring them here walking through his father's well-kept garden so that he can have something new and fresh to look at each day.

A cloud—a very small cloud—passes across the face of the sun; and in the softened light I too am able to look at the Taj without screwing up my eyes.

As the boy said, it does not change. Therein lies beauty. For the effect on the traveller is the same today as it was three hundred years ago when Bernier wrote: 'Nothing offends the eye... No part can be found that is not skilfully wrought, or that has not its peculiar beauty.'

And so, for a few moments, this poem in marble is on view to two unimportant people—the itinerant writer and the gardener's boy.

We say nothing; there is really nothing to be said. (But now, a few months later, when I try to recapture the essence of that day, it is not the monument that I remember most vividly. The Taj is there of course; I still see it as a mirror for the sun. But what remain with me, more than anything else, are the passage of the river and the sharp flavour of the Ashok fruit.)

In the afternoon I walk through the old bazaars which lie to the west of Akbar's great red sandstone fort, and I am not surprised to find a small street which is almost entirely taken up by kite-shops. Most of them sell the smaller, cheaper kites, but one small dark shop has in it a variety of odd and fantastic creations. Stepping inside, I find myself face to face with the doyen of Agra's kite-makers, Hosain Ali, a feeble old man whose long beard is dyed red with the juice of mehendi leaves. He has just finished making a new kite from bamboo, paper and thin silk, and it lies outside in the sun, firming up. It is a pale pink kite, with a small green tail.

The old man is soon talking to me, for he likes to talk and is not very busy. He complains that few people buy kites these days (I find this hard to believe), and tells me that I should have visited Agra twenty-five years ago, when kite-flying was the sport of kings and even grown men found time to spend an hour or two every day with these dancing strips of paper. Now, he says, everyone hurries, hurries in a heat of hope, and delicate things like kites and daydreams are trampled underfoot. 'Once I made a wonderful kite,' says Hosain Ali nostalgically. 'It was unlike any kite seen in Agra. It had a number of small, very light paper discs trailing on a thin bamboo frame. At the end of each disc I fixed a sprig of grass, forming a balance on both sides. On the first and largest disc I painted a face and gave it eyes made of two small mirrors. The discs, which grew smaller from head to tail, gave the kite the appearance of a crawling serpent. It was very difficult to get this great kite off the ground. Only I could manage it.

'Of course, everyone heard of the Dragon Kite I had made, and word went about that there was some magic in its making. A large crowd arrived on the maidan to watch me fly the kite.

'At first the kite would not leave the ground. The discs made a sharp wailing sound, the sun was trapped in the little mirrors. My kite had eyes and tongue and a trailing silver tail. I felt it come alive in my hands. It rose from the ground, rose steeply into the sky, moving farther and farther away, with the sun still glinting in its dragon eyes. And when it went very high, it pulled fiercely on the twine, and my son had to help me with the reel.

'But still the kite pulled, determined to be free—yes, it had become a living thing—and at last the twine snapped, and the wind took the kite, took it over the rooftops and the waving trees and the river and the far hills for ever. No one ever saw where it fell. Sahib, are you listening? The Dragon Kite is lost, but for you I'll make a bright new poem to fly.'

'Make me one,' I say, moved by his tale, or rather by the manner of its telling. 'I will collect it tomorrow, before I leave Agra. Let it be a beautiful kite. I won't fly it. I'll hang it on my wall, and will not give it a chance to get away.'

It is evening, and the winter sun comes slanting through the intricate branches of a banyan tree, as a cycle rickshaw—a different one this time—brings me to a forgotten corner of Agra that I have always wanted to visit. This is the old Roman Catholic cemetery where so many early European travellers and adventurers lie buried.

Although it is quite probably the oldest Christian cemetery in northern India, it has none of that overgrown, crumbling look that is common to old cemeteries in monsoon lands. It is a bright, even cheerful place, and the jingle of tonga-bells and other street noises can be heard from any part of the grounds. The grass is cut, the gravestones are kept clean and most of the inscriptions are still readable.

The caretaker takes me straight to the oldest grave— this is the oldest known European grave in northern India—and it happens to be that of an Englishman, John Mildenhall. The lettering stands out clearly:

Here lies John Mildenhall, Englishman, who left London in 1599 and travelling to India through Persia, reached Agra in 1605 and spoke with the Emperor Akbar. On a second visit in 1614 he fell ill at Lahore, died at Ajmere, and was buried here through the good offices of Thomas Kerridge, Merchant.

During the seventeenth and eighteenth centuries, the Agra cemetery was considered blessed ground by Christians, and the dead were brought here from distant places. Thomas

Kerridge must have put himself to considerable expense to bury his friend in Agra. Mildenhall was a romantic, who styled himself an envoy of Queen Elizabeth. Unfortunately he left no account of his travels, although a couple of his letters are quoted in the writings of Purchas, another English merchant, who lies buried in the Protestant cemetery a couple of furlongs away.

Nearby is the grave of the Venetian, Jerome Veronio, who died at Lahore. According to some old records, he had a hand in designing the Taj, modelling it on Humayun's tomb in Delhi. There had for long been a belief that this 'architect' of the Taj lay buried in the cemetery but no one knew where. Then in 1945, Father Hyacinth, Superior Regular of Agra, scraped the moss off a tombstone, revealing the simple epitaph: 'Here lies Jerome Veronio, who died at Lahore.'

Actually, there is no evidence that Veronio designed the Taj, and even if he had something to do with it, he was only one of a number of artists and architects who worked on its construction. The chief architect was Muhammed Sharif of Samarkand. Each drew a salary of one thousand rupees per month. Ismail Khan of Turkey was the domemaker. A number of inlay workers, sculptors and masons were Hindus, including Manohar Singh of Lahore and Mohan Lai of Kanauj, both famous inlay workers.

A man of more authentic accomplishments was the Italian lapidary, Horten Bronzoni, whose grave lies at a short distance from Veronio's. He died on 11 August 1677. According to Tavernier, it was Bronzoni who cut the Koh-i-noor diamond; and, says Tavernier, he cut the stone very badly.

Bronzoni is again mentioned as having manufactured a model ship of war for Aurangzeb, who had been annoyed by the depredations of Portuguese pirates and was anxious to create a navy. The ship was floated in a huge tank and manoeuvred by a number of European artillerymen. It made a ridiculous sight and convinced the Emperor that a navy was out of the question.

There are over eighty old Armenian graves in the cemetery, but the only one that interests me is the tomb of Shah Azar Khan, an expert in the art of moulding a heavy cannon. One of these, 'Zamzamah', earned a measure of immortality in Kipling's *Kim*—'who holds *Zam-Zammah*, that 'fire-breathing dragon', holds the Punjab, for the great green-bronze piece is always first of the conqueror's loot.' The gun was 14.6 feet long, and is still at Lahore.

Other historic tombs lie scattered about the cemetery, but the most striking and curious of them is the grave of Colonel Jon Hessing, who died in 1803. It is a miniature Taj Mahal, built of red sandstone. Although small compared to a Mughal tomb, it is large for a Christian grave, and could easily accommodate a living family of moderate proportions. Hessing came to India from Holland, and was one of a colourful band of freelance soldiers (most of them deserters) who served in Sindhia's Maratha army. Hessing, we are told, was a good, benevolent man and a great soldier. The tomb was built by his wife Alice, who it must be supposed, felt as tenderly towards the Colonel as Shah Jahan felt towards his queen. She could not afford marble. Even so, her 'Taj' cost a lakh of rupees.

Outside, in the street, people move about with casual unconcern.

Street-vendors occupy the pavement, unwilling that their rivals should take advantage of a brief absence. In the banyan tree, the sparrows and bulbuls are settling down for the night. A kite lies entangled in the upper branches.

THE DARYAGANJ STRANGLER

Summertime. The hotel was full, the mall road crowded. Mussoorie was enjoying its annual invasion of holiday makers, eager to escape the heat and dust of the cities of the plains. The hill station thrived on its visitors; and the visitors thrived on the clear sky and bracing air of the Himalayan foothills.

Miss Ripley-Bean and Mr Lobo were enjoying a mid-morning coffee break in the shade of the huge deodar that had been planted in front of the Royal Hotel when it had opened just over a hundred years ago. The late Mr Ripley-Bean had been one of its founders, and his daughter, an elderly spinster, was the legal occupant of two small rooms in a corner of the tennis court block. She was now seventy, but 'full of beans' according to everyone who knew her. Mr Lobo, the hotel pianist and sometimes assistant manager (whenever managers were on leave, which happened frequently), enjoyed the old lady's company, even though he was almost half her age. She reminded him of a favourite aunt in Goa.

This balmy summer morning they were discussing the activities of the Daryaganj strangler.

Daryaganj was a historic area of Delhi, part commercial, part residential, linking New Delhi to the old city. In the times of the Mughals it had been known for its elegant villas, with their views of the winding Yamuna River. Now it was an overcrowded locality, a clutter of shops, offices, homes and vehicles ranging from cars to motorcycles to handcarts.

'This serial killer,' said Miss Ripley-Bean, 'why does he operate in this particular area—why not Paharganj or Jor Bagh?'

'I've no idea,' said Mr Lobo. 'Probably lives in Daryaganj. And if he's the sort of killer who likes to prowl around at night, he will probably feel at home on familiar streets.'

'And his victims—what were they like? Did he take anything from them?'

'It seems not. A woman was found strangled in the driver's seat of her car. Her expensive rings and necklace had not been touched. A businessman found on the street outside his office still had a roll of banknotes in his pocket. More than one woman was killed—several men—all the victims quite prosperous, but nothing stolen.'

'Interesting,' said Miss Ripley-Bean, 'And now—at least, according to the papers—there has been a pause in his activities. No victims for over a month.'

'Perhaps he's dead. Or taking a break. On holiday, like everyone else,' ventured Mr Lobo.

'Well, let's hope he doesn't come to Mussoorie for his holiday. Or stay at the Royal,' said Miss Ripley-Bean. 'We are quite full, aren't we?'

'Almost,' said Mr Lobo with a grin. 'Except for that room

just next to yours. The haunted room.'

It was Miss Ripley-Bean's turn to smile. 'I make sure it's haunted, you know. Just to ensure I don't get a noisy neighbour. And it does give me the shivers whenever I look through the window. I keep seeing that poor man hanging there—Mr Manohar—the manager who hanged himself. It seems he was in debt all over the place, and falsifying the hotel accounts.'

Here there was a distraction. Fluff, Miss Ripley-Bean's Tibetan terrier, emerged from beneath a bench, barking furiously, and set off in hot pursuit of a couple of monkeys that had been trying to get into one of the rooms.

'These monkeys are really too many now,' observed Miss Ripley-Bean. 'Soon they'll be occupying the ballroom and the kitchen. But I'm wondering—this Daryaganj strangler—could he perhaps be among us already, enjoying his holiday? This hotel is packed with people— might he be one of them?'

'What an alarming thought!' said Mr Lobo.

The Daryaganj strangler was indeed taking a break, not because he had lost his appetite for strangling people he disliked, but because his last intended victim, a resourceful editor of a women's magazine, had managed to break two of his fingers before he could get a firm grip on her throat. She had then kicked him in the groin and made her escape—in time to bring out the next issue *of Women's Realm* right on time.

Our strangler now had two of his fingers in splints, having told his doctors that he had jammed them in the door of his car.

Yes, he had a car, a pretty red Ford Fiesta, and he was now driving it up to Mussoorie for a much-needed holiday. The splints had gone, the fingers were healing fast and his palms were itching to be put to use again.

Miss Ripley-Bean was woken from her afternoon siesta by the short inquiring barks of Fluff. Someone had finally occupied the room next door. But it wasn't until late evening that she caught a glimpse of her neighbour. He was a small, wiry man wearing thick-lensed spectacles who peered around him in the gathering gloom, trying to get his bearings. He had a slight limp.

To Miss Ripley-Bean he did not look like someone who could strangle a child, let alone an adult; but then she noticed his hands. They were large, long-fingered hands, almost like a musician's; even Mr Lobo did not have such large hands.

It wasn't until the following morning that Miss Ripley-Bean met her neighbour. He was sitting on a bench not far from the tennis court block, and he was flipping through the pages of a bound manuscript. Miss Ripley-Bean was returning from a brisk morning walk, Fluff at her heels. The stranger looked up at her approach. She gave him a friendly good morning, and he acknowledged her greeting with a little nod. He did not smile. He was a serious person who seldom smiled.

'You look like a scholar,' observed Miss Ripley-Bean, always curious about people's occupations.

'A novelist,' said the scholar, holding up his manuscript. *'The Great Indian Love Story.'*

The little man on the bench did not look like a great lover, but then, thought Miss Ripley-Bean, you never could tell with men. Sometimes these skinny, undernourished types turned out to be sexual gymnasts! Thoughtfully, she placed herself on a garden seat opposite the newcomer. No one's going to attempt to make love to me, admitted Miss Ripley-Bean to herself, but I don't like the look of those hands—or the way they keep twitching!

'I've always wanted to meet a novelist, but that isn't the same thing, is it?'

'No,' said the novelist, with a look of contempt. 'Do you read novels?'

'Only crime stories,' confessed Miss Ripley-Bean. Agatha Christie and Mary Roberts Rinehart."

'Poor stuff. You ought to read my novel.'

'Well, as soon as it's published, I shall get a copy for myself.'

'Published! But no one will publish it!'

'Why not?'

'It's far too good for them!' The young man was getting agitated. His mouth twitched, the veins stood out on his forehead. 'They don't know anything about writing, the publishers we have today! All they want is soppy love stories or self-improvement books or financial scandals or how to get rich overnight. Money, money, money!'

Well, I suppose it makes the world go round. Could do with a little myself. Maybe your book will make you rich too!'

'It will, if someone publishes it.'

Miss Ripley-Bean promised to read the manuscript, and the young author looked quite pleased; he was no longer agitated.

'My name is Roshan Puri,' he said. 'You will hear of me one day.'

Miss Ripley-Bean did not see Mr Puri for two or three days. There was a lock on his door and he was still the official occupant, having paid a week's rent in advance. But no one seemed to know where he had gone. This wasn't unusual. Sometimes residents took off for a day or two, visiting Rishikesh or one of the pilgrim destinations higher up in the mountains.

Miss Ripley-Bean read the novel, or tried to read it. It did not make much sense to her. In places it read like Barbara Cartland, in places like Lobsang Rampa, in others like Kahlil Gibran, and she suspected that the writer had lifted large portions of his book from their works. In the novel, the hero has a double, a Hitler-like character who rules the world with an iron fist; but our hero, with a little help from a slave girl, gets rid of the dictator and takes his place, bringing peace and prosperity to all nations. The hero also happens to be the author.

'Not a bad idea,' mused Miss Ripley-Bean, 'except that it's all such a muddle. Mad, quite mad!'

On the third morning of Mr Puri's absence, Mr Lobo walked over with the morning newspaper.

'Has our Nobel Prize candidate returned?' he asked.

'No sign of him,' said Miss Ripley-Bean. 'But he left his window open, and the monkeys have been in and out.'

'Tearing up his manuscript, no doubt. Well, there's a publisher found dead in Dehradun, just outside the gate of his house. Seems he'd gone out for an after-dinner stroll;

he's been strangled with an electrical cord. Could it have been our guest?'

'I hope not. I'd rather the Daryaganj strangler confined his activities to Daryaganj.'

'I hear all the publishers are moving out to Gurgaon. Some of them are keeping dogs!'

'Well, we're not publishers, are we, Fluff?' Miss Ripley-Bean gave Fluff a ginger biscuit, which was consumed with relish.

'Well, take care, Aunty May,' said Mr Lobo, departing. 'And let me know when he gets back.'

Mr Puri turned up at teatime, looking quite spry, refreshed and pleased with himself.

'He looks quite harmless,' thought Miss Ripley-Bean.

Fluff didn't think so. He growled at the approach of their neighbour.

'So did you get a chance to read my book? Don't you think it's a masterpiece?'

Over the years, Miss Ripley-Bean had learnt to be diplomatic with vain young men. They were apt to go off the handle if you made fun of them.

'Most interesting,' she said. 'I couldn't put it down. Here's the manuscript, and I wish you luck with it. But don't leave it lying around; the monkeys are a great nuisance.'

'And so are publishers,' he said quite venomously. 'I believe there's one staying in the hotel.'

'Not that I know of,' said Miss Ripley-Bean. 'But then I wouldn't know. I'm not on the hotel staff, nor am I a paying customer. My late father ran this hotel once, and when he sold it, I was given this corner to live in. It was part of the arrangement. I've been here most of my life, and believe me, there are stories to tell. Perhaps I should write a book too!'

But Mr Puri wasn't impressed. As far as he was concerned, there was only one author in the world worth reading, and that was Roshan Puri.

But he was right about the publisher. There was indeed one staying at the hotel: Cyrus Piranha, the genial, rotund owner of Chalta Hai Books.

Cyrus had made his fortune producing playing cards with erotic motifs and had got into trouble once or twice for flouting the obscenity laws. Now he was acquiring respectability by publishing 'literature'—mostly English translations of erotic Chinese, Japanese, Indian, Arabic and Madagascan classics. The fortune had doubled, and Cyrus usually took his holidays in Bermuda or Switzerland, where he had stashed away some of his wealth for a 'rainy day'. He was slumming in Mussoorie this time simply in order to please his wife who had once studied at Stockwood, one of the posh schools on the hillside.

Cyrus was not in the least interested in seeing an unpublished writer's first novel—he left such chores to his editors—but he was in a good mood, enjoying the climate and the company in the Royal's bar—so he smiled affably at the young man who thrust a manuscript into his lap and said, 'Here's your next bestseller, Mr Piranha. Read it while you are here—it will be an unforgettable experience!'

From then on, Cyrus's visit to Mussoorie became one long unforgettable experience.

Miss Ripley-Bean looked on with some amusement as the obsessed young writer went about stalking, and sometimes pouncing upon the unfortunate publisher.

Mr Piranha did, in fact, skim through the manuscript, but the love scenes were obviously second-hand, lacking in masala, and he sent it across to Roshan Puri's room with a note saying, 'Not our kind of book. Why not try Champagne Press?'

Roshan had already tried Champagne Press, whose managing editor had recently been found strangled to death in one of those small guest houses that proliferate around Ansari Road, Daryaganj. In fact, Roshan had been rejected by almost every publisher in the capital, he had taken his revenge on quite a few of them; the publisher of Chalta Hai Books would not get off so easily!

A period of stalking ensued. Wherever Cyrus Piranha went, Roshan would follow, albeit at a discreet distance. Miss Ripley-Bean couldn't help noticing Roshan's agitation whenever he caught sight of the publisher ambling across the lawns and pathways surrounding the old hotel. The grounds were extensive and it could take about half an hour to circle the property on foot. She repeated to herself in an undertone:

Mary had a little lamb,
Its fleece as white as snow,
And everywhere that Mary went,
The lamb was sure to go.

'You are always quoting nursery rhymes,' observed Mr Lobo, joining Miss Ripley-Bean for a cup of tea.

'Great truths in nursery rhymes. They capture the spirit of the times.'

'Ancient times or modern times?'

'Both. Human beings haven't changed all that much. Greed and envy and love and hate continue to ride piggyback on our shoulders like the ghost in those tales of Vetaal.'

'And what happened to Mary's little lamb?'

'I'm not sure, probably turned into roast lamb with mint sauce. Isn't that on the hotel's menu for today? A speciality of the Royal.'

Roshan Puri decided to make one final attempt at convincing Cyrus Piranha of the virtues and great potential of his book. Most writers see themselves as geniuses, even when others don't, and Roshan had greater conceit than most. And in his insane moments had he not become a superhuman eliminating some unworthy members of the human race?

Cyrus Piranha went for a walk on that fateful day. Not too long a walk: around Camel's Back, past the cemetery and as far as Lover's Leap—a promontory on the edge of a cliff crowned by a hawa-ghar, an open pavilion where strollers could sit and gossip.

Hill station legend had it that a pair of young lovers, ostracized by society and driven from their homes, had committed suicide by leaping to their death from this particular spot. It was a long drop—about a hundred feet—to the rocks below. There was nothing by way of bushes or shrubbery to impede one's descent.

But that had been a long time ago, and in the recent past no one had made the leap.

It was a beautiful summer's day, and Miss Ripley-Bean had also gone for a walk, accompanied by Fluff. But they took the upper road, the path that went over the brow of the hill, past the old church and a disused tennis court. Resting there on a bench, she could see the road below and the pavilion at Lover's Leap.

There were no lovers in sight, just two men having a heated argument. Miss Ripley-Bean could make out Roshan Puri's high-pitched voice, raised in anger, but she could not make out what he was saying. The other man could be Cyrus Piranha, but Miss Ripley-Bean couldn't be sure because he stood in the shadows, his back to the pavilion wall. She could hear him laugh from time to time. Yes, it was Cyrus's boisterous laugh.

Suddenly, Roshan made a lunge at his tormentor, arms outstretched. The bigger man stepped back, raising his walking stick. He could not back away too much because the wall was behind him, but Roshan stood in the open, no wall or railing behind him. He was leaping about like a dervish, trying to get at Cyrus's throat. Cyrus kept him at bay with the walking stick. They moved back and forth, like a couple of sparring stag beetles. Then the walking stick shot out, catching Roshan in the midriff. He let out a howl, stepped back, slipped on a carpet of pine needles and went over the edge of the cliff.

A faint thud, and then silence. Two or three passers-by gathered at the spot, looked over the edge. Cyrus was busy explaining things. Down on the rocks a dead man lay, his vacant eyes staring up at the noonday sun. Did he fall or was he pushed? No one could be certain. Even Miss Ripley-Bean wasn't certain, but she hurried back to the hotel, Fluff at her heels, to inform Mr Lobo and others of the tragedy.

So it was all an accident, it appeared. And Roshan Puri had no family or close relatives to come poking around and making a fuss. There was a post-mortem of course, which listed the poor fellow's injuries, and as it was midsummer, the body was cremated without delay.

'Do you think he was the strangler?' Mr Lobo wondered. 'He seemed harmless enough.'

'Except for those large hands,' said Miss Ripley-Bean. 'And we shall know in time, depending on whether or not the population of Delhi publishers continues to decline...'

But Cyrus Piranha was still his jovial self. He had of course seen Miss Ripley-Bean on the hilltop that fatal day, but he wasn't sure just how much she had seen. Nor had she given him any indication of her thoughts or suspicions.

The day before he was due to leave, he presented her with a bottle of wine and asked her if there was anything he could do for her. It appeared that he had taken a liking to the old lady during his brief but eventful holiday.

'Well, there is something you *can* do for me,' said Miss Ripley-Bean after a moment's thought. 'You see, I'm writing this history of the hill station—the Queen of the Hills is over a hundred—and it's full of interesting people and things that have happened over the years. Famous visitors, memorable events, lovers' leaps, and even the odd murder... Well, it's time I started looking for a publisher

'Say no more, my good lady!' interrupted Cyrus. 'Consider

me your publisher. My office will send you a contract, and before I go I will leave a small cheque with you by way of an advance.'

And true to his word, Cyrus presented Miss Ripley-Bean with a cheque for five thousand rupees, which at the time happened to be the highest advance ever received by a first-time author from a publisher in India.

And what happened to Roshan Puri's masterpiece? The forgotten manuscript lay in that unlucky, unoccupied room for several weeks, until one day the room-boy came across it, took it home, gave it to his friend who worked in the tea shop down the road, who gave it to the owner of the shop, who got his daughter to fashion paper bags out of those hundreds of foolscap pages, and then used the paper bags for selling peanuts and channa to his customers.

This of course was in the days before plastic bags came into use. And before frustrated geniuses could publish their masterpieces online!

REUNION AT THE REGAL

If you want to see a ghost, just stand outside New Delhi's Regal Cinema for twenty minutes or so. The approach to the grand old cinema hall is a great place for them. Sooner or later you'll see a familiar face in the crowd. Before you have time to recall who it was or who it may be, it will have disappeared and you will be left wondering if it really was so-and-so…because surely so-and-so died several years ago…

The Regal was very posh in the early '40s when, in the company of my father, I saw my first film there. The Connaught Place cinemas still had a new look about them, and they showed the latest offerings from Hollywood and Britain. To see a Hindi film, you had to travel all the way to Kashmere Gate or Chandni Chowk.

Over the years, I was in and out of the Regal quite a few times, and so I became used to meeting old acquaintances or glimpsing familiar faces in the foyer or on the steps outside.

On one occasion I was mistaken for a ghost.

I was about thirty at the time. I was standing on the steps of the arcade, waiting for someone, when a young Indian male came up to me and said something in German or what sounded like German.

'I'm sorry,' I said. 'I don't understand. You may speak to me in English or Hindi.'

'Aren't you Hans? We met in Frankfurt last year. You look exactly like Hans.'

'Maybe I'm his double. Or maybe I'm his ghost!'

My facetious remark did not amuse the young man. He looked confused and stepped back, a look of horror spreading over his face. 'No, no,' he stammered. 'Hans is alive, you can't be his ghost!'

'I was only joking.'

But he had turned away, hurrying off through the crowd. He seemed agitated. I shrugged philosophically. So I had a double called Hans, I reflected; perhaps I'd run into him some day.

I mention this incident only to show that most of us have lookalikes, and that sometimes we see what we want to see, or are looking for, even if on looking closer, the resemblance isn't all that striking.

But there was no mistaking Kishen when he approached me. I hadn't seen him for five or six years, but he looked much the same. Bushy eyebrows, offset by gentle eyes; a determined chin, offset by a charming smile. The girls had always liked him, and he knew it; and he was content to let them do the pursuing.

We saw a film—I think it was *The Wind Cannot Read*— and then we strolled across to the old Standard Restaurant, ordered dinner and talked about old times, while the small band played sentimental tunes from the 1950s.

Yes, we talked about old times—growing up in Dehra, where we lived next door to each other, exploring our neighbours' litchi orchards, cycling about the town in the days before the scooter had been invented, kicking a football around on the maidan, or just sitting on the compound wall doing nothing. I had just finished school, and an entire year stretched before me until it was time to go abroad. Kishen's father, a civil engineer, was under transfer orders, so Kishen, too, temporarily did not have to go to school.

He was an easy-going boy, quite content to be at a loose end in my company—I was to describe a couple of our escapades in my first novel, *The Room on the Roof*. I had literary pretensions; he was apparently without ambition although, as he grew older, he was to surprise me by his wide reading and erudition.

One day, while we were cycling along the bank of the Rajpur canal, he skidded off the path and fell into the canal with his cycle. The water was only waist-deep; but it was quite swift, and I had to jump in to help him. There was no real danger, but we had some difficulty getting the cycle out of the canal.

Later, he learnt to swim.

But that was after I'd gone away...

Convinced that my prospects would be better in England, my mother packed me off to her relatives in Jersey, and it was to be four long years before I could return to the land I truly cared for. In that time, many of my Dehra friends had left the town; it wasn't a place where you could do much after finishing school. Kishen wrote to me from Calcutta, where he was at an engineering college. Then he was off to 'study abroad'. I heard from him from time to time. He seemed happy. He had an equable temperament and got on quite well with most people. He had a girlfriend too, he told me.

'But,' he wrote, 'you're my oldest and best friend. Wherever I go, I'll always come back to see you.'

And, of course, he did. We met several times while I was living in Delhi, and once we revisited Dehra together and walked down Rajpur Road and ate tikkis and golgappas behind the clock tower. But the old familiar faces were missing. The streets were overbuilt and overcrowded, and the litchi gardens were fast disappearing. After we got back to Delhi, Kishen accepted a job in Mumbai. We kept in touch in desultory fashion, but our paths and our lives had taken different directions. He was busy nurturing his career with an engineering firm; I had retreated to the hills with radically different goals—to write and be free of the burden of a 9-to-5 desk job.

Time went by and I lost track of Kishen.

About a year ago, I was standing in the lobby of the India International Centre, when an attractive young woman in her mid-thirties came up to me and said, 'Hello, Rusty, don't you remember me? I'm Manju. I lived next to you and Kishen and Ranbir when we were children.'

I recognized her then, for she had always been a pretty girl, the 'belle' of Dehra's Astley Hall.

We sat down and talked about old times and new times, and I told her that I hadn't heard from Kishen for a few years. 'Didn't you know?' she asked. 'He died about two years ago.'

'What happened?' I was dismayed, even angry, that I hadn't heard about it. 'He couldn't have been more than thirty-eight.'

'It was an accident on a beach in Goa. A child had got into difficulties and Kishen swam out to save her. He did rescue the little girl, but when he swam ashore he had a heart attack. He died right there on the beach. It seems he had always had a weak heart. The exertion must have been too much for him.'

I was silent. I knew he'd become a fairly good swimmer, but I did not know about the heart.

'Was he married?' I asked.

'No, he was always the eligible bachelor boy.'

It had been good to see Manju again, even though she had given me sad news. She told me she was happily married, with a small son. We promised to keep in touch.

And that's the end of this tale, apart from my brief visit to Delhi last November.

I had taken a taxi to Connaught Place and decided to get down at the Regal. I stood there a while, undecided about what to do or where to go. It was almost time for a show to start, and there were a lot of people milling around.

I thought someone called my name. I looked around, and there was Kishen in the crowd.

'Kishen!' I called, and started after him.

But a stout lady climbing out of a scooter rickshaw got in my way, and by the time I had a clear view again, my old friend had disappeared.

Had I seen his lookalike, a double? Or had he kept his promise to come back to see me once more?